THE MARRIAGE MISSION

SWEET MARRIAGE OF CONVENIENCE ROMANCE

THE MARRIAGE MISSION SERIES
BOOK ONE

SHANAE JOHNSON

THOSE JOHNSON GIRLS

CHAPTER ONE

*T*he familiar grip of tension seized Noah Henri as he surveyed the landscape. The air was thick, laden with the residue of battles past, each corner shadowed with potential dangers. It was a scene of neglect, a territory where chaos reigned supreme, untouched by the hand of order for what might have been eons.

Noah wasn't big on hyperbole, which he knew the word *eons* to be. The building hadn't stood for an indefinite period of time. It was thirty years old, having been erected the same year he was born. The exterior was well kept and inviting. But on the inside, it was dark and twisted.

Huh. So maybe it was a bit more like him than he'd originally thought.

His eyes, trained to spot danger in its many forms, immediately honed in on the enemy—wires, like coiled serpents, sprawled haphazardly across the battlefield. They twisted around aging machinery, their frayed and exposed innards a loud witness to the ravages of time and inattention. It was a mine-field of electrical hazards, each step potentially his last.

The smell of the frontline enveloped him—a mix of burnt offerings and the acrid tang of grease, lingering like the ghost of assaults long finished. The sounds of the last stand, though absent, echoed in his mind: the clang of pots and pans, the sizzle of meat on the grill, the frantic calls of comrades in arms. This kitchen was no place for the faint-hearted. The equipment, veterans of countless meals, stood worn and weary, their once gleaming surfaces dulled and scarred by the skirmishes of daily service.

With a thud, Noah dropped his work bag on the floor, surprised to find it gleaming enough to eat off of. Not that he would. He knew this restaurant, Chow Town, came with a bunch of stars given from people who sat on the other side of the wall every night in this small town. He had come in through the back. The door had been opened by one of his military brothers.

"It's not pretty in there. But I knew you were the man for the job." That was all Fish had said.

Sergeant Min-ho Pike was a man of few words, which was likely why Noah didn't mind returning to the man's company. He wasn't one for company these days, either. Not after…

Noah gave a shake of his head, not letting those flashes of memories invade his mind. Flashbacks were the walking nightmares of veterans.

"You good, Henry?"

"Yeah, Fish."

"Let me know if you need anything. Gotta get back to the vegetables."

It was still odd to hear the big man say things like that. Noah was used to watching Fish handle heavy weapons of machine guns, mortars, and anti-tank weapons. Now he was chopping potatoes and carrots. That knife did look sharp enough to garrote a man, though.

"Just stay out of Chef Chou's way," Fish called as he palmed the knife.

"Is he here?"

"She. And yes, she's always here."

"But don't worry," called another line cook. "The lights will flicker and there'll be a loud boom before she appears."

3

The other cooks and workers chuckled. But quietly. As though they believed the walls were listening.

Fish wasn't laughing. The man looked dead serious. Back in their Army days, they'd had fierce female drill sergeants and team leaders, so Noah knew the man had a healthy appreciation for women in leadership. If this woman got under his skin enough to warrant a warning, she must be something else.

Noah turned back to the task at hand. The wiring of the restaurant was packed out of sight behind a wall and also up in a crawl space. He decided to tackle the crawl space first. He'd seen what was behind the wall. He didn't hope for any more organization than the disarray he'd already seen.

Disorder was an anathema to someone like him. As an EOD specialist who handled explosives, Noah liked order. Thrived on it. Things were either black or white. Ones or zeros. Live wires or duds.

Up in the crawl space, his movements were deliberate, mindful of the booby traps hidden in the shadows. The strategy was clear: assess, dismantle, rebuild. He would need to marshal all his skills for this operation, every lesson hard-earned in the field now critical. His hands, steady despite the adrenaline, were ready to defuse the situation, to bring order back to this forsaken place.

He had been hired not as a soldier but as an electrician, brought in to tame the wild, outdated wiring, to make this restaurant safe for the civilians who enjoyed the fare. The irony wasn't lost on him—a man who had faced down the threat of real bombs now tasked with defusing the metaphorical ones lurking in the walls of a small-town eatery.

Better this than having lives in his hands again. Better to work alone than forge any new friendships. Even though the people in this small town kept trying, despite his only having been here for two days.

The desk clerk at the hotel continued to try and make small talk with him, seemingly undeterred by Noah's grunts or silence. The teen at the gas station eyed him with open curiosity and big eyes like a puppy hoping for a scratch behind the ears. Even Fish was friendlier than usual. Noah had actually gotten a few sentences out of him when the man had been mostly silent the whole five years he'd known him before. What was with this place?

He didn't care. He wasn't going to stay around long enough to find out. He'd get this job done. Pack his stuff and move on. Jack Reacher style.

Except Noah carried around more than a toothbrush. And he was vain enough to want a few changes of clothes that he kept in a suitcase. And he drove a new Ford truck instead of hitchhiking or taking buses. Other than that, he had no attachments. Couldn't afford them. Not after.

He gave another shake of his head to ward off the flashes of memory. Then Noah set to work. The battlefield inside the crawl space transformed before his eyes, from a zone of danger to an orderly grid. It would take another crew three weeks to do the job. Working alone, after hours, it would take Noah a week. Ten days tops. He was that good.

Noah knelt among a tangle of wires under the dim glow of his flashlight, tools spread out around him like a surgeon's instruments. The air was rich with the smell of brewing coffee and the early whispers of cinnamon. He was focused on the wiring, the quiet click of his wire strippers slicing through the silence, when the sound of a frustrated voice drifted up toward him.

The voice was smoky. It curled in the air. He could've sworn he could breathe it in. It was likely the fumes.

"You don't have to worry about a thing."

A tingle pressed against his shoulder blade. He rolled the muscles there, and it released.

"I'll take care of it, Nãinai. Yes, I promise."

The tingle went to the other side of Noah's shoulder. This time, when he tried to roll it free, it spread toward his spine. He knew that word *Nãinai*. He'd traveled a lot during his time in the service. It was the Mandarin word for grandmother.

"No, I don't need a man to do it for me. I can handle it."

The smoky voice was irritated. It made Noah grip his wrench. He imagined her down there, brow furrowed, phone pressed against her ear, perhaps standing in the midst of her own battlefield— juggling phone calls with the precision of a general. He couldn't see her, but her presence filled the space, her determination palpable.

"Please, let's not have this conversation again. This is not feudal China. And I'm not some piece of property to be handed off like the emperor giving away land to lords. No man is getting his hands on my restaurant."

Noah's grip tightened on the screw he'd loosened. For some odd reason, he wanted to pocket it. Take it home with him and keep it with him at all times.

Distracted, his attention divided, Noah failed to

notice the precarious angle at which his tool hovered over the open wiring. His mind was in two places at once—caught in the wires before him and tracing the lines of an unseen woman's resolve. It was in this split second of inattention that his tool slipped, making contact where it shouldn't.

The resulting zap was immediate, a sharp, sizzling protest from the wires that made him jerk back. The lights below flickered, a strobe of warning before a muffled boom filled the air, more startling than destructive, but enough to plunge the kitchen into sudden darkness.

Heart hammering against his ribs, Noah cursed softly under his breath. This was not how he operated, not how he wanted to start his first day on the job. He scrambled down and out of the crawl space.

And then she was there.

It was still dark, but her blonde hair was like a beacon of light beckoning him forward. His fingers uncurled around the screw. It clattered to the ground as he reached out to touch, remembering too late that he didn't yet have the right to take her into his arms.

CHAPTER TWO

The morning rush at Chow Town had barely begun, yet Jacqui Chou already felt the weight of the day pressing down on her. She was sharing part of her kitchen with the bakery next door. That bakery happened to be her baby sister's shop, and Jules was not the best at sharing. Not when her parents had given the youngest of the three Chou siblings everything while they lived.

Jacqui didn't begrudge her baby sister that treatment. Not when she continued to model the behavior long after their parents' deaths.

"You need a man to help you."

Not for the first time today, Jacqui wished her dad was still here. Jun Chou was the only man she trusted to shoulder any of her burden. It had been hard to keep her back straight these last three years that he'd been gone.

"No, I don't need a man to do it for me. I can handle it."

"Why are you modern women so proud? Men and women have distinct roles. Men hunt and women gather. Woman aren't built for battle. It's causing too much stress in this day and age as women pick up the mantle."

Jacqui rolled her eyes, glad her grandmother couldn't see it. Words Meiying Chou would argue, but not unseen gestures. Sassy words had gotten Jacqui many a swat on the backside when she was little. She doubted her grandmother would stop now that she was in her eighties.

"You need to get married. Have a man help you shoulder some of the burden. What about that nice boy, Richard, from down the street?"

Jacqui didn't remind her grandmother that she was already dating someone.

Wait a minute... she was dating someone.

Wasn't she?

Mason had texted her over a week ago, trying to arrange a date so they could talk. Had she responded? She thought she had... hadn't she? But she couldn't remember if she'd received a text back from him. And they hadn't gone on that date to talk. She should check her phone to see if she'd put something on her calendar app. But her grandmother was still talking in the receiver.

"He's an accountant. He could take over the books while you work the kitchen."

Jacqui's fingers curled around her A5 journals. Her bullet journals did not make her tax preparer happy. But they made Jacqui happy. It was the best relaxation for her, putting invoices in purple and tracking expenses with various shades of pink—not red. There was just something about bringing order and putting items in categories that soothed her soul.

"Please, let's not have this conversation again, Nāinai. I do not prescribe to the Confucian ideology of the Three Obediences."

The notion of a woman obeying first her father and then her husband and finally her sons during widowhood was laughable in this third generation Chinese-American family, where the ratio of women outnumbered the men by at least four in each generation. Nāinai and her sisters had run roughshod over their father as well as their sons. Still, there were some cultural customs that survived over an ocean and over time.

"Don't take that tone with me. It's not exactly your restaurant. I still have controlling shares. I'll hand them over when you and your sisters are married."

Jacqui pinched the bridge between her nose. This restaurant had been her grandfather's. Though he'd been outnumbered, Ming Chou still did believe that men should be in charge. It was likely his only defense inside this matriarchal battlefield. Meiying had been on the matriarchal side while her husband was alive. Her walls came down completely when she lost her son. Now it would seem that she would only hand the reins off to another man. But there were no other Chou men to take over.

Jacqui opened her mouth to remind her grand-mother of that fact when she heard it. There was a fizz. Then a crackle. Then a boom. The line went dead, and the lights went out.

She didn't have the money for this. She didn't have the patience either. Just as she didn't have the nerves to deal with her Nãinai about getting married to have a man take over the day-to-day worries. Chow Town was her heart and soul, but today it felt like a puzzle whose pieces just wouldn't fit.

The stress coiled tightly in her chest, a constant companion she wished she could shake off. In a flurry of frustration and paper, Jacqui stormed out of her office, her mind a cyclone of receipts, reservations, and relentless regulations.

Her pace was swift. So caught up in her whirlwind of thoughts, she didn't see him—a veritable wall of man—until she collided with his broad, solid chest. The impact was like hitting a pillar, immovable and unexpectedly comforting.

The surprise sent a jolt through her, disrupting the storm inside. For a fleeting second, she found herself enveloped in warmth and safety, his arms steadying her against him. His presence was commanding yet gentle, a harbor in the midst of her tempest.

"I've got you."

She should've moved. She had no idea who this was. It wasn't one of her crew. No one would have dared.

He was too big to be one of her sisters. And they were both, well, women.

He was too broad and strong to be Mason. And Mason smelled like expensive cologne. This man smelled like... well, a man. He was earthy and musky. She wanted to curl up against him.

"I'm so sorry, I didn't see—" Jacqui began, her words trailing off as she lifted her gaze to meet his.

His eyes were a calm, steady force, locking on to hers with an intensity that peered right through to her frazzled soul.

"No harm done. Are you okay?" His voice was deep, a smooth rumble that resonated within her, soothing the edges of her frayed nerves. Jacqui allowed herself to lean into the comfort he offered, her body unconsciously responding to the stability his frame provided.

In that brief pause, wrapped in the unexpected sanctuary of his hold, a wild, reckless thought flickered through her mind—what if she could just stay? What if she could hand over the tangled mess of worries and fears weighing her down? There was an unspoken promise in his steadiness that he could bear the load, that perhaps, just for a while, she wouldn't have to carry it all alone.

The thought was a dangerous one, a fleeting fantasy in a world that had taught her the hard lessons of reliance and loss. Jacqui knew better than to depend on anybody but herself. Dependence was a vulnerability, a risk she couldn't afford. Everything she had built could be taken away in an instant, leaving her with nothing but the remnants of misplaced trust.

With a resolve born of necessity, Jacqui jerked

out of his hold, stepping back into her reality of independence and control. "Who are you?"

He tipped an invisible hat. "Noah Henry."

"Two first names? What are you, a catfish?"

"Is that a chef joke?"

"Men on social media trying to scam old ladies always have two names."

Noah chuckled, and the sound rumbled through Jacqui. She needed to put more distance between herself and this man.

"Everything okay?" It was her sous chef. Fish eyed the two of them with a raised brow. It was the most expression Jacqui had ever seen on the man's face.

Jacqui did step back then. She could not appear weak in front of her staff, which was mostly men. She was a female chef and restauranteur in a male-dominated field. They could not see her vulnerable.

"This is the electrician I hired," said Fish.

"Really? Is this how you work? You blow things up?"

Something twitched in Noah's eye before he blinked. "Your wires are so crossed it was inevitable. You need a complete overhaul."

"Maybe I should start with you."

"Are you firing me?"

There was something in his voice, something that

screamed at her to run back into his arms. Jacqui took a step forward, but only because she was not the kind of woman to back down. Now, was she prepared to launch herself at him or *launch* herself at him? She would never know because Fish stepped in between them.

"Nobody can do it faster and better than Henry."

"If she doesn't want me, I'll leave," said Noah.

Jacqui did not want him to leave. Which was probably why he should.

"Jed's Grits and Grub has been opened for a month now, and it's impacting dinner service. We're already running at two-thirds our capacity. Henry will have us up in two weeks. Anyone else will take three at best."

Gone was the soothing sense Jacqui had gotten from Noah Henry. Gone was the tender look in his eyes. What replaced it was a cocky expression. She needed him, and he knew it. Which meant he was going to take advantage at some point. He could try, but she would be dogging his every step. If she could manage to find the time to do it.

"Fine," she said.

"Fine," he said.

"Just don't screw anything else up. I'm headed

out. Food prep needs to be done by the time I get back. I will be checking everyone's work."

Jacqui marched out the back door. It wasn't until the cool morning breeze wafted up her nostrils that she realized she was holding her breath. Noah Henry's scent had made her dizzy and lightheaded. The feeling didn't pass as she headed down the street.

CHAPTER THREE

𝒩oah found his gaze following Jacqui as she left the kitchen. She looked as good going as she had coming. Those curves of hers were silhouetted, swaying as she easily picked her way through the people and appliances in the dim lighting, like she knew this place like the back of her hand. Noah's fingers twitched at his sides, a reflexive urge to reach out, to pull her back into the circle of his arms where they had shared an unexpected connection.

She'd fit perfectly against him. He swore he'd heard a lock click into place. Or more likely the zing when he cut a wire. If he had acted on that impulse to pull her back to him, it would've likely been like cutting the wrong wire. Somehow, the thought of an explosion between himself and Jacqui Chou didn't sound like a bad idea.

She was prickly, that much was clear. The type of woman who wore her independence like armor, who likely viewed men as either obstacles to be navigated or tools to be used in the pursuit of her goals. He wouldn't mind her stepping on him in those heels to get a leg up. In fact, his lower back warmed at the prospect.

As Jacqui's retreating figure disappeared from view, the atmosphere in the kitchen noticeably shifted. The tension that had coiled tight around the space began to unwind. One by one faces appeared, shoulders were turned and profiles revealed. Bodies came out of the dark recesses of the kitchen as staff started to filter back in, their expressions all bright with relief.

"Man, I wasn't sure you were going to survive that." A brown-skinned woman with a braid woven around the crown of her head dusted her hand on her pristine apron. "Most folks get fired before they even know what hit 'em. She usually fires first and asks questions later—or sometimes, she doesn't bother asking at all."

"Guys, this is Noah. He's an old Army buddy. He'll be working on the electrical." Fish stepped up to make the introductions. "This is Nia. She's in charge of the fry station. And Aarav is the saucier. Behind you is Elena at the grill station. And Liam is the prep cook."

A bubbly brunette winked at Noah, while a young man who looked like he couldn't have graduated high school gave Noah a chin lift greeting.

"You missed Larry," said Aarav. "He was fired last week when Chef caught him using the wrong sauce in the Kung Pao Chicken. He was out the door before dinner service even started."

That seemed a big error to Noah. Seemed Larry got what he deserved if he couldn't follow instructions, which is what a recipe was.

"And that waitress Sarah," Elena added as she flipped meat on the grill, "mixed up the dessert orders during the Valentine's rush. I've never seen Chef so mad. Sarah didn't last the night."

Seemed to Noah that Sarah should not have been a waitress. When wires got crossed, bad things happened. Sarah was lucky it was sugar and not trinitrotoluene that she mixed up. That powdery substance better known as TNT made things go boom.

The stories continued, each one painting a picture of Jacqui's stern leadership and zero-tolerance policy for mistakes. Yet as Noah listened, he felt a growing respect for the woman they all referred to as Chef. Like she was Madonna or Cher. Leading a busy team where people's lives were in their hands required discipline. Food could nourish, but it could also kill.

As the horror stories swirled around him, Noah found himself more intrigued than deterred. Chef Jacqui's approach, though harsh, appeared to stem from a place of passion for her craft and a desire for excellence. There was a fire in Jacqui, a relentless drive that matched his own experiences in the military. Where others saw a boss quick to judge and dismiss, Noah saw a leader pushing her team toward greatness, albeit with a heavy hand.

The way her staff shared tales of survival under her regime clearly bonded them in a way only those who've faced the same battle could understand. The men and women widened their circle, allowing Noah to become part of it. Noah took a step back.

"I'd better get back to it," he said. "Catch you later, Fish."

"All right, Henry."

"Wait," called Nia. "Your name's Noah Henry?"

"Two first names," said Elena. "Sounds too good to be true. Just like a catfish."

Elena gave him another wink. The steam rising to her face would've made another woman look tired and frazzled. It cast a glow about her features. Noah wasn't interested.

Too bad Elena wasn't done. "You're the bomb expert? So that's why you survived meeting Chef Jacqui, huh?"

"Yup," said Noah, taking another step back. "Which is why I need to get back to it."

"Just know she's a bomb waiting to happen. If you need shelter, I'm just over here."

"Right." Two more steps and he was out of the kitchen.

Noah heard the laughter and camaraderie of the staff behind him. He didn't hear Fish's voice, but he knew his presence was there. There had been a time when that kind of talkativeness and chiding happened in their unit. But that was before it all blew up. It was no wonder both of them had gone quiet.

He didn't need any new friends. Certainly not a girlfriend. His past still clung to him, a shadow that followed each step he took toward a new life in this small town. But as he passed by the open door of the chef's office, his gaze involuntarily swept inside, and something within caught him off guard.

The office was a small, well-lit space just off the kitchen's main hustle. Pens and pencils were sorted meticulously in cup holders, organized by color—a rainbow of functionality. Papers weren't just stacked; they were aligned with precision, each one either filed away in labeled folders or placed in strategic lines on the desk, as if they were soldiers on parade. There was a calm, controlled aura to the room that resonated with Noah. It soothed the part of him that was frayed—the same part that craved structure in the chaos of life.

Drawing his eyes away from the serene office, Noah turned his attention to the task that had brought him here: the wiring. Where Jacqui's office was a realm of order and calm, the wiring behind the restaurant's main service panel was a tangled mess of neglect, a snarled web of cables that reminded him of DIY home renovation nightmares. Cords snaked over and under each other in a haphazard fashion. Colors blurred together in a muddled confusion that made his fingers itch for order.

Noah knelt down, tools in hand, and began the meticulous process of detangling and reorganizing. Each wire was to be traced back to its source, tested for integrity, and labeled for future maintenance. As his hands worked, his mind, which had been clouded

24

with the remnants of past battles and recent loneliness, began to clear. The physical act of sorting, stripping, securing, and sleeving the wires became a meditation. Here, in the solitude of his work, he wasn't a former soldier with a troubled past; he was just a man, fixing what was broken one wire at a time, finding a new purpose in the simple, satisfying work of restoration.

CHAPTER FOUR

*J*acqui's heels clicked against the tiled floor of the small receiving room. The rhythm of her pacing matched her racing heart. She paused outside the office door but didn't touch the handle. Instead, her gaze locked in a silent battle with Trudy, the receptionist seated behind her cluttered desk. The air between them crackled with tension, an unspoken rivalry that had become a ritual over countless visits.

Trudy was under the false impression that the woman on the other side of that closed door was her best friend. Trudy was wrong. It was just that the door wasn't on Jacqui's side today.

The clock on the wall ticked away, each second stretching out, amplifying the suspense that hung heavy in the corridor. Jacqui shifted her weight from one foot to the other, her posture rigid, ready to spring into action the moment she got her chance. Trudy, seemingly unfazed, met her stare with an icy resolve, her fingers poised above her keyboard like a gunslinger ready to draw.

The office door finally swung open. It reminded Jacqui of those late night science fiction movies she and Bunny would watch during sleepovers where neither girl would sleep after seeing the ill-fitting, poorly imagined, yet still nightmarishly realistic costumes of the space aliens. The spaceship's door would always open with a whoosh of smoke, perhaps to indicate a change in atmosphere.

The closed office door opened, releasing a wave of air-conditioned coolness into the tense hallway. Both Jacqui and Trudy leaped forward. It was a mad dash, a split-second race fueled by a childish rivalry. And Trudy, who had been on the track team in high school, made it there first. The tall woman blocked Jacqui's way with a smirk.

From within the office, a voice cut through the tension, authoritative yet amused. "Let her in, Trudy."

Jacqui didn't bother hiding the triumphant, albeit smug, look she shot Trudy as she breezed past the receptionist. She loved the fact that the once star of the track was now sitting still in an office chair. Victory was sweet, even in these small battles. Stepping into the sanctuary of the office, her demeanor softened immediately upon spotting Bunny, her lifelong friend, first cousin, and now city official, standing by the window with a knowing smile.

"Hey, BFF," Jacqui said loud enough to be heard on the other side of the closed door.

Bunny quirked an eyebrow. "What are you, five? You have got to get over this feud with Trudy."

"Just tell her I'm your best friend."

"You're my best friend."

"Wait, let me open the door so she can hear you."

"Jacks, what do you need, babe? I'm up to my eyeballs in city business. We've got a water main break on Third that's causing chaos. The budget revisions are due by Friday, and I just got off the phone with a very upset resident about the new park zoning. I'm juggling like five meetings today. So what's up?"

Looking at Bunny was like looking into a mirror. Well, sort of. Where Jacqui's hair was blonde from her mother's side, Bunny's hair was a deep brown from her African American mother. They'd both inherited their fathers' eyes. Jacqui's dark eyes called to her father's Chinese ancestry while Bunny's pale grey eyes called to her father's Swedish heritage. Their smiles were almost identical. Likely because Jacqui's mom and Bunny's dad had been siblings.

Bunny's presence commanded attention, not through volume but through the quiet confidence she carried, a confidence born of being the eldest in a family of girls, of having shouldered responsibilities far beyond her years. It was a trait Jacqui knew well. They were two sides of the same coin—leaders by necessity, overachievers by nature.

Beyond the exterior, beyond the accolades and achievements, Jacqui saw her best friend. The girl who, like her, had spent her childhood looking after her younger siblings, juggling homework with household chores, and dreaming of a future where their efforts would bear fruit. Bunny's successes, much like Jacqui's, were not merely personal victories but a tribute to their shared ethos of hard work, determination, and the silent promise to lift as they climbed.

"I need you to put on your accountant hat for a minute."

Bunny raised her right eyebrow at the request. "Did you not hear the part where I balanced the city's budget last week? A job that belongs to the mayor. Yet he says there needs to be revisions."

"You should be mayor."

Bunny raised the other brow.

"It's... it's been tough, Bun. The wiring's a nightmare, the city's on my back about code violations, and don't get me started on the staff turnover."

"I can't change the city code for you. No matter how much I depend on you for my meals."

The warmth in Bunny's words wrapped around Jacqui like a comforting embrace, reminding her that despite the battles she faced daily, she wasn't alone. The strength she drew from her friendship with Bunny was a beacon guiding her through the storm.

"And I'm willing to bet the turnover isn't all the staff's fault."

Did she say beacon? Scratch that. Her bestie was more like the storm. "If only I could find competent people."

"If only you would give mediocre people a chance to become better."

"Let them cut their teeth in somebody else's kitchen and come to mine when they're polished."

Bunny smiled. "Give me your spreadsheets."

Jacquie kept her face straight. She'd thought it

would take more arm twisting to get Bunny to agree. But like her, Bunny didn't like to waste time. Jacqui pulled her bullet journal out of her purse.

"No." Bunny held up her hands. "If you pass me that bujo, I will find some actual bullets to shoot you with."

"You know I'm allergic to Excel."

"Maybe that's the reason you're an accounting nightmare."

Jacqui lovingly placed the bullet journal on her friend's desk and petted the cover. "This is what relaxes me."

"Stickers and colored pencils won't get you out of this mess."

"I'm not in a mess. Dad left the money. It's Nãinai that won't release it to me or my sisters. She thinks we need to be married."

"So get married. Haven't you been dating Jason for a few months?"

"Mason. And I'm not sure we're dating any more. He hasn't returned my texts."

"In how long?"

Jacqui shrugged. She'd meant to look at the text back in her office. Then she'd gotten distracted by the lights. Then there had been that mishap with the electrician and all his muscles.

Wait. What were they talking about again? Oh yeah, whether or not she was still dating Mason. She'd figure that out later.

"I just need to find the money to get the rewiring done. The guy has already started. And I can't tell him to stop because I need the job done. I can't keep using Jules' kitchen. A bakery kitchen can't handle my menu."

Her sister's bakery was a new addition and had the proper, up-to-code rewiring done. Jacqui had used her profits to take care of her baby sister first. She was still funding the middle sister Jami's dreams of being a world traveling food critic. But Jami's traveling served Jacqui's business when her sister came back with exotic dishes to add to the menu. And Jami technically worked for Chow Town by supplying all of the desserts.

"Thankfully, I still have access to your online account." Bunny let out a low sigh as she tapped on her desktop keyboard.

"I have an online account?"

"You don't have the money to spare. You're one disaster away from it getting ugly. You've used up all of your credit. Maybe if you call Jami home, then—"

"No, I'm not doing that."

It was a testament to how much Bunny knew

Jacqui that she didn't argue. Bunny gave her younger siblings the world, too. Meanwhile, she worked her fingers to the bone in a thankless job for an unqualified playboy mayor.

"Okay, maybe we can move some other things around," said Bunny.

As they delved into the specifics, plotting a course through the bureaucratic red tape and discussing potential solutions for the restaurant's challenges, Jacqui felt a glimmer of hope. She just also had to hope there wouldn't be any disasters on the horizon.

CHAPTER FIVE

$\mathcal{N}$oah knelt down, his toolbox open beside him, as he examined the network of wires hidden behind the walls of the restaurant. The task ahead, which he had initially anticipated to be a daunting overhaul, was turning out to be less of a challenge than expected. Whoever had installed the wiring twenty years ago had clear knowledge of what they were doing. The job just hadn't been updated since then.

With his flashlight in hand, Noah peered closer, assessing each connection and junction box. The wiring, though outdated, had been laid out with a precision that spoke of a time when people took pride in craftsmanship. It was a far cry from the haphazard, often reckless installations he'd encountered in his military career, where urgency often trumped accuracy.

A buzzing in his pocket had him pulling out his phone. He flipped the top open and had to wait a moment for the graphics to load. Though Noah liked his wiring up to date, he preferred to keep on hand one of the oldest models of cell phones. Finally, the screen on the flip phone updated to reveal a series of text messages. The letters came through okay, but then there were boxes around question marks as the latest emojis had no place to land in his outdated device.

Being kept out of the emoji loop didn't bug him. Noah smugly watched as his friends frantically updated their phones until the devices were no longer of use, and they'd have to go buy a newer model. Not him. If it ain't broke, don't fix it might apply to his phone, but it wouldn't work with the wiring. The county would fine the restaurant if it didn't do the updates. Noah not getting emojis wouldn't hurt anyone. A wire misfiring because it was out of date could kill.

Looking down at his phone, he saw more letters. Those letters formed words. The word bubbles popped up, moving quickly as different people on the text chain chimed in. The text thread announced a reunion for the remaining members of his old unit.

A tremor went through Noah's fingers. He balled his hand into a fist until the trembling stopped. He held on to the clench, refusing to let the memories take form at the front of his mind.

Noah tapped at the face of the phone until the mute conversation feature came up. His thumb hovered over the choices: mute for an hour, mute for the day, mute indefinitely. He chose indefinitely and slid the phone back into his pocket.

Once the chatter on his phone was silenced, his mind returned to quiet. Once his mind returned to quiet, Noah got back to work. Once he got back to work, he saw the path to the finish line for this job. He'd beat his estimated completion date by at least a few days.

The realization that his time in Chow Town would draw to a close sooner than anticipated cast a shadow over his work. The prospect of leaving, of not seeing Jacqui's fiery determination and passionate focus in action, filled him with an unexpected sense of regret. Each glimpse of her, whether issuing commands in the kitchen or navigating the challenges of running a restaurant, had drawn him in, revealing layers of her character that intrigued him more with each passing day.

"You could come home."

The voice was Jacqui's. She sounded like an angel, but she lured him like the devil. He could follow her. It wasn't as though he had a home to go to. He spent his days working jobs. His nights were spent in cheap hotel rooms or on campgrounds. He preferred not having a place to belong. But if that space came with the amenities of Jacqui Chou's smoky voice, he might never check out.

"I know you're working hard, but it's just that I miss you so much."

Noah took another step toward that voice. He wouldn't have admitted it first, but he'd somehow missed her, too. She hadn't been far from his mind since that first encounter. His fingers still held the memory of her flesh in his. It was a sensation he didn't think he'd ever forget.

"No, no, no. It's nothing like that, sweetie."

Sweetie? Jacqui was on the phone with a sweetie? A growl emanated through the space as Noah envisioned his hands around the neck of any man that dared get close to Jacqui.

"Wait, Jami, I think I hear a dog."

Noah pressed his back to the wall as Jacqui came out of her office, cellphone pressed against her ear. It was a newer model. Likely the most up to date so that she could talk to Jami and get all the emojis. Including the new ones with cats with heart eyes.

"I must be hearing things. James, babe, I know you're out there living your dream. And you're doing so much for the restaurant, bringing back authentic recipes and regional ingredients. I just think it would be nice to have my sister home."

It was her sister. Sweetie-babe was Jacqui's sister. The tightness that had formed in Noah's chest loosened its grip.

"No, no, no, everything is fine."

Noah noticed every time Jacqui said *no* three times, her voice pitched a little higher. It sounded like she was reaching for the panic button to him.

"The restaurant is great. Jules is great. I'm great and… Nāinai? Oh, she's… great."

Another high-pitched panic sounded on that last word. Noah remembered Jacqui speaking on the phone with her grandmother about a man getting his hands on the restaurant.

"No, no, no. Everything's great."

She was lying. She was in his line of sight now. He could tell a lie when he saw it, as well as when he heard it.

Noah's military background had honed his observational skills, making him particularly adept at noticing the subtle tells that someone might be lying. As Jacqui came into his line of sight, speaking animatedly into her phone, her body language spoke volumes to him, even if her words were meant to obscure the truth to her sister on the other end of the line.

There was the rapid tapping of her foot, a rhythmic and unconscious motion that betrayed her nervous energy. Her fingers were twisting a strand of her hair, winding it around her index finger repeatedly then releasing it only to start again. Every so often, her eyes would flick upward, as if seeking validation or the right words from the ceiling.

Perhaps the most telling, however, was the way she bit her lip at the end of her sentences, chewing on it briefly as if to hold back the real words she wanted to say. This action, combined with slight hand gestures that seemed to swat away an invisible annoyance, painted a clear picture for Noah: Jacqui was definitely not telling the truth.

"You don't worry about a thing. Just enjoy

Shanghai and send lots of pictures. I love you, too. Bye."

Jacqui pressed the phone to her forehead. Noah wanted to smooth out the worry lines there.

She was in some kind of a bind. Noah's mind worked to unravel the cause, much like methodically tracing the path of tangled wires to find the source of a short circuit. It was a bind that had to do with a man and her restaurant and her grandmother.

He should stay out of it. He should leave her to defuse her own situation. If he went in and tugged at the wrong wire, it could very well blow up in his face.

Noah couldn't help himself. He made his way to the open door of her office. Reaching overhead, he pressed his palms into the top of the doorframe and leaned into the room. His shoulders were so broad they filled the entire frame.

She didn't open her eyes. He didn't rush her. He took the moment to look at her, fighting the urge to go to her and scoop her into his arms.

Jacqui must have heard his desires. She opened her eyes then. Anger was the first thing he saw as she fixed on his eyes. Then, as she fixed on his chest, that anger melted, and Noah saw want. He felt her gaze like a caress as she looked at his chest, like she wanted to fling herself against it. But when she looked again at his eyes, that desire snuffed out.

The woman wanted him. She needed him. Noah was going to give her exactly what she needed. He took a step toward her—and then the lights went out.

CHAPTER SIX

*J*acqui ran her hand over the worn bullet journal that served as her ledger. No matter how many colors she used or how much Washi tape she bordered the numbers with, the money just wasn't there.

Maybe Bunny was right. Maybe she should embrace spreadsheets. But Jacqui knew the computer would tell her the same thing as her inked notes. She was in a hole.

The call with Jami had ended as she feared, with laughter and gentle refusal, her sister's wanderlust proving insurmountable even in the face of Chow Town's financial strain. Not that Jami knew about the financial strain. And if Jacqui had her way, neither of her sisters would ever know the weight she was drowning under.

This was her responsibility. Her father had left her in charge of her sisters with his dying breath. Their dreams had to come before hers. Jules had gotten her updated kitchen before Chow Town, and Jami would travel the world, tasting all of its foods on Jacqui's dime.

Jacqui's heart ached, not just for the loss of potential savings, but for the distance that seemed to stretch ever wider between her and her siblings. Even though Jules was just next door, her baby sister had drawn a line in the sand. That line she insisted her hovering sister was not allowed to cross so that Jules could run her business on her own.

The notion that her diabetic little sister wanted to be a pastry chef had been one thing. Then to open a bakery had been another. Though in all honesty, the bakery was in better financial straits than the restaurant with its low overhead and small staff of one.

Though Jacqui suspected Fish helped out here and there behind her back. Lucky for her sous chef that it was Jacqui's sister he was cheating on her kitchen with. Even more lucky that the pastries he helped with were desserts for the restaurant.

Jacqui looked back down at her ledger. Her mind whirled with calculations and schemes, each more desperate than the last. The food bill was paid for the month. The utilities weren't due until the middle of the next month. The only thing on the immediate horizon was the electrical work. And that shouldn't come due for at least two weeks, probably more if this electrician was like all the other workers underestimating their time, only to admit they'd need more later. Noah Henry was bound to encounter delays, forcing the project to extend and thus buying her time until the next influx of cash at the month's end. It was a flimsy hope, she knew, but hope was a currency she was running short on.

Lost in her thoughts, Jacqui started when she looked up to find Noah framed in her doorway, his arms braced against the frame, a casual stance that belied the strength she knew lay beneath. The reason she knew about that strength was because she'd felt it full force when he'd held her in his arms.

A jolt of something warm and unsettling fluttered in her stomach, memories of their unintended embrace flooding back with unexpected intensity. For a moment, amid the chaos of her responsibilities, she had found an oasis of peace in his arms. His presence now, standing there as if he were the guardian of her own personal haven, reignited that flicker of tranquility.

It was ludicrous, Jacqui chided herself, to think that any part of her troubles could be soothed by the mere proximity of a man she barely knew. And yet, the idea of leaning on him, of sharing the burden that had been hers alone since her parents passed, was tantalizing.

Noah was probably here to deliver bad news, for the announcement of a delay that she both dreaded and desired. He was going to demand more money from her. She steeled herself for the request at the same time as she chided herself for hoping he might be different.

Noah took a step forward. He was still so broad that she couldn't see past him beyond to the kitchen. His presence was so big that he shut out the hum of the appliances.

She got the notion that nothing would get past this man if he didn't want it to. Not the bills. Not the food critics or unhappy customers. Not her grandmother and her outdated notions. Not even her sisters looking to her for answers.

Jacqui swallowed the desire that surged in her throat from wanting that moment of quiet. That moment of not coming up with a solution. That moment of not being responsible for voicing a plan of attack.

Noah opened his mouth to speak.

Jacqui opened her mouth to cut him off.

And then everything went dark.

They were alone in the restaurant. The morning shift hadn't started yet. She'd only known he was here by the work bag he'd left near the door. She supposed Fish had let him in and gone next door to the bakery to do his prep.

The sudden plunge into darkness enveloped her office like a thick blanket, snuffing out the light in an instant. Jacqui's heart lurched, the abrupt loss of visibility sending a jolt of surprise through her. But before she could even gasp, she felt strong arms wrap around her, a familiar and unexpectedly comforting embrace enveloping her in warmth and security.

In the cocoon of Noah's arms, Jacqui found herself doing something she hadn't done in a long time—she relaxed. The ambient noise of the kitchen faded, replaced by the sound of their synchronized breathing. She closed her eyes, allowing herself a momentary escape, a fleeting surrender to the peace that radiated from Noah's very being.

"That's likely the light fixtures." Noah's voice

broke the silence, his tone practical yet soothing. "They're probably going to need to be updated along with the new wiring."

His words, meant to be reassuring, instead served as a splash of cold water, jerking Jacqui back to the harsh light of reality—even if that light was metaphorical at the moment. "Oh, so you're going to charge me for that, too?"

"No, I know a workaround that'll hold. But eventually, you'll have to upgrade. My solution will buy you time."

In the darkness, she imagined his expression, certain she would find no hint of opportunism in his gaze. Jacqui's emotions were a whirlwind, caught between gratitude for his immediate solution and the dread of future expenses.

"I'll be done with the wiring ahead of schedule, so I can take on that unneeded day to do the fix. No extra charge," he added, as if reading her mind.

The roller coaster of her emotions dipped once more, the relief of saving some pennies now overshadowed by the realization that payment for his services was looming closer.

As the lights flickered to life, casting a dim glow over the office, Jacqui stepped back from Noah's embrace, the spell of the darkness broken. The return to visibility felt like a return to their respective roles—chef and electrician, employer and contractor—yet something had shifted.

"Thank you, Mr. Henry. I appreciate your efficiency."

"Call me Noah."

Jacqui bit her lip.

Noah's hooded gaze latched on to the movement. "You let me know if you need anything else."

Jacqui got the impression he'd give her whatever she needed. "Just efficiency in your work."

He gave her a smirk and then backed out of her office. But he didn't get far. Jules was behind him.

"My power just went out. Jacks, my pastries will melt."

Jacqui pinched the bridge of her nose.

"Sounds like your circuits are overloaded," said Noah.

"Who are you?" Jules eyed him with interest.

"He's—" Jacqui began, but Noah cut her off to introduce himself to her younger, pretty sister.

Jules' jet black hair was chopped into a playful pixie cut, while her pale, almost ethereal eyes were a haunting echo of their mother. She was small and petite, her delicate frame moving with a grace that belied a certain fragility, an almost damsel-like quality that seemed to draw protective instincts from those around her. Especially men.

There was an almost instinctive desire to shelter her, to shield her from the world's harsher edges. This was in sharp contrast to Jacqui herself, who stood tall and robust, her presence commanding and sturdy, shaped by years of leading a busy kitchen and managing a business. Where Jacqui was a pillar of strength, Jules seemed like a whisper of silk.

"I'll come over and take a look," said Noah.

Before Jacqui could say anything, like she didn't have the money to pay him for it, or Jules had bad breath in the morning, Noah was gone. He walked calmly, capably as though the problem was already solved.

CHAPTER SEVEN

*N*oah crouched beside the hulking form of the bakery's malfunctioning refrigerator, his tools spread out on the floor like a surgeon's array beside an operating table. The sweet aroma of baking pastries mingled with the tang of electrical work. As he peeled back the access panel, his eyes quickly took in the condition of the wiring within. It was pristine, nothing like the tangled mess he had encountered in Chow Town. However, as his trained gaze swept over the neatly arranged wires, he spotted several telltale signs of corner-cutting.

Cheap, mismatched wire nuts, a few overly stripped wires, and sloppy electrical tape wraps that spoke of haste rather than heed. It was clear that while the outward appearance had been polished, the essential, underlying work was fraught with compromises. He made a mental list of the materials he would need and the adjustments that had to be made.

Fish stood next to him, though *stood* was a generous term for the way the other man's attention drifted from the fridge to the front of the shop, where Jules, the pretty baker and Jacqui's sister, flitted between customers like a fairy doling out ambrosia.

"You know, I'm starting to think I should charge by the hour for distraction as well as electrical work."

"What?" Fish cocked his head toward Noah but didn't take his eyes off Jules.

That was until Jules turned. When she did, Fish's gaze hit the floor, and he busied himself inside Noah's tool box. Jules smiled brightly, her features reminding Noah of her sister. The younger woman was pretty, to be sure. Jules sparkled, but Jacqui was a bright flare Noah didn't want to shield his eyes from.

"How's it going in there?" Jules asked. "Will you be able to save me?"

"Yes. Absolutely. Definitely." All these assertions

came from Fish, who was holding a hammer, which would do nothing for all the wires.

"Just let me know what you need and my sister will get it for you."

Noah frowned at that. He'd seen the worry lines around Jacqui's eyes. He'd heard the catch in her voice when she'd spoken with her other sister about money.

"What I need is a voltmeter." Noah looked pointedly at Fish.

Fish bobbed his head like he was caught on a hook. He made no move to reach for the tool.

"Fish?"

"Yeah?"

"The meter? Unless you want her pastries to turn into soup."

Fish passed the tool, but his gaze was inevitably drawn back to Jules. "Right, right. Having Jules' pastries melt would be a crime against humanity."

Jules gave Fish a distracted smile. Then that pixie face of her scrunched into worry as she looked at her creations in the cooling refrigeration unit.

The inside of the fridge was a mess of wires and cooling coils, a puzzle that Noah was methodically working through. "Looks like the compressor's overheating. We need to reset it and see if that fixes the immediate issue."

With a click and a whirr, the refrigerator hummed back to life, the gentle cold air a sign of victory. Noah stood, wiping his hands on a rag. "There. She should hold now, but you'll want to get that part replaced soon, along with cleaning up the wiring, or it'll happen again."

"Do I have to hire someone new? Or can you take care of it?" asked Jules.

Noah had to bite his tongue before he barked that no one else would be taking care of anything but him. Not when he'd seen the mess in Chow Town. And this building was not only attached to the restaurant, it was just on the other side of Jacqui's office.

It was a relatively simple fix. For him, at least. He wouldn't put it past another technician to charge the Chou women an arm and a leg. "I'll take care of it."

There went that warm smile again. One thing about this Chou sister, she gave her smiles more freely than the eldest. Noah knew Jacqui was the eldest without meeting the other sister. Jacqui had oldest sister vibes blaring from her pores.

"Like I said, my sister will take care of the money stuff. But in the meantime..." Jules turned and pulled something from the fridge. "Cherry danishes all around?"

"Just glad I could help," Noah said, taking the proffered treat. "Whoa, that hit the sweet tooth."

"It's monk fruit."

"Monkey fruit?"

"No, monk fruit is a plant that's used in place of sugar. I'm diabetic. All of my baked goods are sugar free and keto friendly. Much better for you and they all taste good, too."

Noah couldn't deny that last bit. The cherry danish had a lightness to it along with the sweet notes. If she hadn't have told him there was no sugar, he wouldn't have believed it. His estimation of the pretty baker rose.

As they watched her go, Fish let out a wistful sigh. The big man cradled the pastry as though it was a precious gift from an angel.

"She's amazing, isn't she?" hedged Noah, counting off attributes on his sticky fingers. "Beautiful. She can cook. And that smile."

Fish's smile fell from his face. Noah had seen the man in combat. His eyes would go glassy, like a tiger's. Fish had the eye of the tiger look right now.

Noah clapped his friend on the shoulder,

laughter in his voice. "Just messing with you, man. She's all yours."

"She's not mine. She has a boyfriend. Manchild is more like it."

"I agree with you there, young man."

It wasn't normal for anyone to sneak up on Noah, or Fish for that matter. Behind them stood an elderly woman. Her silver hair, the only traitor of her years, flowed like a river of moonlight, contrasting sharply with her otherwise youthful appearance.

She reminded him of the famed actress Michelle Yeoh. Like the actress, there was an unmistakable strength in this woman's posture, her back arrow-straight, betraying a lifetime of carrying not just physical burdens but the weight of her experiences and wisdom. It was her gaze, however, that captured Noah's full attention—a shrewd, penetrating look that seemed to see right through him, assessing his character with a precision that felt almost military in its accuracy.

Watching her, Noah was struck by the sense of quiet authority she wielded, a matriarchal figure who commanded respect not through volume but through the sheer force of her presence. It was clear she was the kind of woman who had navigated life's challenges with resilience and grace, shaping her into the formidable yet approachable figure she was today. That's how he knew she was Jacqui's relative. That and the Asian traits were clear in her features.

"My apologies, Mrs. Chou," said Fish, his gaze once again on the ground. "I meant no disrespect."

"I must say, it's rare to see young men so handy these days. And well mannered, too. You both carry yourselves like military men. Am I right?"

This must be the Nãinai that Jacqui had been speaking to on the phone.

Fish straightened up, offering a respectful nod. "Yes, ma'am. We both served."

"My husband was in the military. A good man. It taught him many things, most importantly how to be reliable and strong—not just in body, but in character. Traits that I see in both of you. Traits that make for good husbands."

Noah felt a flush of warmth at the compliment, though the mention of marriage had him inwardly bracing for retreat. When his thoughts drifted to Jacqui, the idea didn't repel him as he expected. In fact, the notion of being someone Jacqui could lean on, of building something lasting, stirred something deep within him.

"Not this again, Nãinai." Jules returned, carrying

a tray with coffee that she offered to both Noah and Fish. "Women today are independent. We don't need husbands. I have my sisters and a group of girl-friends as my support system. I can call a handyman if I need something fixed." She gestured to Noah and Fish. "And I own my business."

"All lovely additions." Mrs. Chou raised an eyebrow, her stance unyielding. "But you won't get your inheritance until you marry."

Jules's response was instant, laced with determination. "I don't need it. I'm doing just fine."

The moment hung in the air, a standoff between generations, when suddenly, the fridge's hum sputtered and died, plunging the appliance—and their conversation—into silence.

The bell over the shop rang. They all turned to the newcomer. It was a lanky man who walked in with shoulders hunched as though he knew he was on enemy territory.

"Not this one," Nāinai sighed. "I thought she dumped him."

"Is that the boyfriend?" Noah asked Fish.

"Not Jules' boyfriend," said Fish. "That's Jacqui's boyfriend."

CHAPTER EIGHT

"Ms. Chou, I'm afraid we've reviewed your application, and at this time, we're unable to extend further credit to Chow Town." The banker's voice was polite but firm, a verbal door closing on her hopes.

Jacqui held the phone tightly to her ear, pacing the small office of the restaurant. She should be checking to make sure that her sister's issues were being handled, but she somehow knew that Noah would take care of it. With that worry freed from her mind, she needed to handle her money issues.

"Surely there's something we can do? I just need a little more time. You know the restaurant is profitable. You've been in here every weekend, Mark."

"I'm sorry, Jacqui, but given the current financials

you've provided and the outstanding debts, it's beyond our risk policy. We truly wish you the best and hope that your situation improves," Mark replied, his tone final. "Can I just check to confirm my reservation for Sunday?"

"You're fine. I'll see you Sunday, Mark." But he wasn't getting an extra helping of dumplings this time.

The silence that followed felt suffocating, the weight of her financial predicament crashing down on her with renewed force.

Jacqui dropped into her chair, staring blankly at the open ledger on her desk. The numbers danced before her eyes, a mocking reminder of her failure to meet the looming bills. There were Jami's travel expenses, and now Jules' refrigerator repair, not to mention the rewiring project, which, while necessary, had accelerated her financial crisis.

Her gaze drifted to her phone, to the draft of a text message that felt more like a surrender than a solution. The idea of reaching out to her boyfriend— or ex-boyfriend, she wasn't quite sure anymore— was a clear sign of her desperation. The thought of proposing marriage as a financial Band-Aid made her stomach turn. What was she going to write? "Let's have dinner so we can discuss getting married so that I can get my inheritance to pay off my bills." The words sounded ludicrous, even in her head. Was she truly that desperate?

Jacqui set her phone down. She couldn't send that message. It went against every principle she stood by, every battle she had fought to prove she could make it on her own. Yet as the reality of her situation settled in, the temptation to find an easy way out gnawed at her resolve.

Needing a moment to clear her head and escape the prison of numbers and failed plans, Jacqui stood and made her way to the bakery next door, hoping the change of scenery and the smell of fresh pastries might offer a break. Or at least something else to worry about.

Jules used the Dexcom app, which allowed family members to share the data and glucose readings of the diabetic loved one. However, Jacqui had been blocked from the app a few weeks ago because Jules felt she was abusing her privileges.

So maybe Jacqui had sent one or two, or maybe dozens, of texts asking what her sister was eating when the readings spiked. And there had been that one time, okay maybe twice, when Jacqui had called ahead to the restaurant she knew Jules and her date were going to to ask the chef about their low glycemic foods. But Jules couldn't bar Jacqui from showing up next door.

As she approached the bakery, Jacqui's steps slowed, her heart skipping a beat when she saw him —her ex—standing in line among the other customers. Was his presence a sign? It had to be. Right?

Jacqui stopped short, her mind racing. Confront him? Turn around?

The chime dinged over the bell as one customer went out. That customer was an old high school friend of Jacqui's, and he greeted her. By name. Before the door closed.

Mason didn't turn. He smiled tentatively at Jules. He was here at the bakery. They couldn't be broken up. Who would go to their ex's sister's bakery?

"Hi, Jules. I'm here to pick up an order. A birthday cake."

Jacqui perked up. Her birthday was coming up. But in a few weeks. The cake wouldn't last that long.

The bell dinged again as someone opened the bakery's door. Jacqui looked down to see her hand on the door. Then her feet moving over the threshold. Was she doing this? Looked like she was.

She looked up to see Mason turn and spot her.

The moment he turned and their eyes met, Jacqui saw the wince that briefly crossed his face.

Compelled by a mix of desperation and a misguided sense of hope, Jacqui moved toward him with an uncertain smile, intent on bridging the gap with a kiss.

Mason, however, misread her approach, extending his hand in a gesture that was meant to be cordial but felt painfully formal. Realizing her intent, he awkwardly shifted to offer his cheek just as Jacqui opted for a hug.

The result was a clumsy dance of misaligned greetings, their bodies bumping into each other in a tableau of discomfort.

The moment was so charged with awkwardness that Jacqui wished she could melt into the floorboards. That's when her eyes landed on Fish, Noah, and Nāinai observing the scene with varying degrees of curiosity, discomfort, and sympathy.

It was the sight of Noah that unsteadied her. He was here to fix the fridge, but what was the growling sound? Was some other appliance on the verge of breaking? All Jacqui saw were dollar signs fleeing from her purse.

"Mason, can we...talk? In my office, just for a

quick chat?" Jacqui managed to say, her voice steady despite the tumult of emotions swirling within her.

Mason hesitated, his glance shifting from Jacqui to the cake Jules was now carefully boxing. Mason snapped up the cake and turned back to her. "I suppose this is overdue."

As they made their way back to Chow Town, Jacqui couldn't shake the feeling of impending doom. The walk was silent, each step heavy with the weight of words left unsaid, of a relationship that had unraveled before either of them had fully grasped the threads.

Once in her office, the door closed behind them, Jacqui turned to face Mason, her heart pounding. Mason placed the cake box down on her desk and lifted his face to hers with a grim set to his mouth.

"We have so much to catch up on," Jacqui tried.

"Catch up on what?"

"On us."

There was that grimace again.

"I'm sorry I didn't immediately return your text messages. We've both been busy. But I want to do better. In fact, I have a proposition." Jacqui took a deep breath. That's when she looked down at the cake box.

"Happy Birthday, My Love—Forever Yours, Mace."

"My birthday isn't for a few weeks." They'd never expressed the L word. They hadn't even shared nicknames. "That's not for me, is it?"

"I've moved on. I thought it was best to make a clean break for both of us."

The room felt suddenly too small, the air too thick. Jacqui's mind raced, her initial intent to reconcile or seek financial salvation from Mason dissolving into the ether. The revelation of his new relationship, symbolized by the cake's tender inscription, rendered her speechless.

"It's not all your fault. We were both busy. But Jill and I, we make time for each other."

"I... I see" was all Jacqui could muster, the words hollow. Her gaze fixed on the cake that represented Mason's future—one that no longer included her. Should she feel sad? Upset? What she felt was... nothing.

Mason reached out, a gesture of consolation, but Jacqui stepped back, a clear sign of the distance that now lay between them. "I should go," Mason said quietly. He reached for the cake, then turned on his heels.

Now what was she going to do? It was a stupid

idea anyway, to think she could marry her way out of a problem. Like a man would solve it for her. She'd have to figure this out on her own, like she did everything.

When she heard Mason gasp, she wondered if he'd changed his mind. If he realized that she was a better choice than... what was the birthday girl's name? But no, a sudden surge of feelings for her wasn't what made her ex take in a breath.

When Jacqui looked up, Noah stood in the door. And he did not look happy.

CHAPTER NINE

*N*oah filled the doorway like a tank on an urban street, cramming itself into a narrow alleyway—completely, leaving no room for doubt. His broad shoulders were a barrier to escape. His fists were clenched, ready to explode on the other man's face.

Mason started when he turned and found the wall of muscle and silent fury. The other man swallowed, then attempted a smile. Failed and attempted a step forward. That failed too.

Noah didn't move, not at first. He looked down at Mason, his gaze hard and unyielding as his body. The moment stretched. The cake teetered in his hands as Mason shuffled uncomfortably, clearly wishing for more room that Noah had no intention of giving.

What had Jacqui seen in this man? If he couldn't manage holding onto a one-tiered cake, how could he have been expected to hang on to the lush curves that were Jacqui Chou? Except the idiot hadn't been trying to hold on to her. He'd tossed her back. Noah had felt that gut-punch as he'd come down the hall.

His thoughts were a storm. Anger churned at the forefront, hot and bitter, for all the ways Mason had just effectively dumped Jacqui. The man had no idea what he'd thrown away.

Aside from being a knock a man down and drag him out into the street's beauty, Jacqui was capable. She was a problem-solver. A go-getter. Clearly, Mason couldn't handle the dynamite that she was.

Then Noah realized that with Mason out of the picture, he could have all those sparks to himself. Noah moved to the side, just a fraction. Mason squeezed through the gap, brushing against Noah with a muttered curse.

As Mason disappeared down the hall and out the door, Noah's gaze lifted to find Jacqui. She stood there, looking lost in the midst of the organized army of paper and folders and clips and pens on her desk.

The sight of her, so vulnerable, reignited Noah's fury like a spark in dry grass. He clenched his fists at his sides. The urge to run after Mason and make him regret his carelessness was a fierce pulse in his veins.

Mason was out of the picture now. And maybe, just maybe, Noah had a chance to show Jacqui how she should be treated. He could coax those embers back into a roaring flame. Maybe he could be the reason she smiled. He hadn't seen it yet, but he somehow knew it would knock him off his feet when it exploded across her face.

"Mr. Henry?" she said when she looked up. Her face didn't break into a smile. It sank into a frown.

"Call me Noah."

"What can I do for you, Mr. Henry?"

"Just wanted to catch up."

One of her brows lowered as though she found his choice of words suspicious. Noah held that gaze. He had the best poker face in the world, mainly because of his former job as an explosives expert. He would love spending the rest of his days poking at the wires of this woman to see which would set her off. Which would defuse her. Which would send off sparks. Which would ground her.

"You mean you want to get paid for completing

your work early?" Her brow creased, letting him know he was on the wrong track.

"I know you're good for it."

The crease it lifted. Like she was relieved. But then she pressed her lips together in what could only be categorized as worry.

"Tell me what you need, Jacqui."

"What I need?" She blinked, and Noah saw a spark of something.

"Yes," he said, stepping closer. "What do you need?"

Her hand came to her throat. Her thumb and index finger pinched at the taut skin of her swan's neck. She bit at the corner of her lip and then swallowed deeply, keeping her lips pressed together as though she was trying to hold something down.

Noah waited patiently. And by patiently, he kept quiet, not saying a word, barely blinking. But he stalked toward her slowly, marking the movements of her throat.

"I need thirty days before I pay your invoice."

"Done." Noah nodded, knowing that that wasn't all. He let the silence drag on, but he didn't let go of her gaze. He took another step toward her until all that separated them was her desk.

"Sixty days would be better."

Noah nodded, watching the sparks in her hazel eyes. He ached to tilt her head back to get a better look. He took another step closer, but all that did was bring him flush against the desk.

Jacqui tilted her head back. When she did, her eyes flashed. "It's not that I don't have it. I do. I just don't have access to it."

"Your inheritance?"

She jerked back as though he had caught that elegant neck between his teeth. Noah had to blink and bite down on his own lip to make sure he hadn't acted on his fantasy.

"How did you know about that?" Then she closed her eyes and grimaced. "Nãinai?"

Noah said nothing. He couldn't. The sparks in her eyes were dancing a new pattern, and it fascinated him.

"My grandfather put that in his will. He was from the old world, where women were basically property. My grandmother could change it, but she agrees with him. She thinks men should be in charge, and women should be at home in the kitchen."

"You've made the kitchen your business."

"Yeah." She grinned. "Me and my sisters have."

Noah grinned too.

Jacqui's gaze dipped to his lips. Then she swallowed and looked away. "Anyway, the inheritance comes with marriage, along with another percentage of ownership in the restaurant. If me and another of my sisters married, that would get us two more percentage points, and ownership would be split evenly between us and Nãinai. If all three of us got married, that would give us controlling interest."

Those two words kept rolling through his mind: *controlling interest*. Noah wanted both from Jacqui Chou; her interest and to make her lose control. He could see it now, her buzzing with excitement.

"I have a proposition."

Jacqui blinked, sparks going off again.

"Marry me."

She laughed. It was an explosive thing. Not of joy. It was a burst of incredulous surprise.

Noah stepped closer.

Jacqui stepped back, the surprise instantly leeching from her face. "That's ridiculous."

"You were going to offer yourself up to that loser." Noah chucked his thumb over his shoulder where Mason had disappeared with his cake.

"You were listening?"

Noah shrugged.

"You are entirely unprofessional. And possibly a stalker."

"Is that any way to talk to your fiancé?"

"You are not. You will never be."

"Fine. Pay up now and I'll be on my way." Noah held his breath. It was a gamble. One he suspected would pay off.

When Jacqui didn't immediately lambast him, he knew he'd won.

CHAPTER TEN

*J*acqui stood frozen, the aftermath of Noah's brazen proposal echoing through the tidy confines of her office. Each word floated around her head, dust in the afternoon sunlight. Any small intake or exhale of breath made the letters flutter. But each time they settled, they formed the same words.

Marry me. But then came *Pay up now and I'll be on my way.* And somewhere in there had been *You were going to offer yourself up to that loser.*

Her mind raced, teetering between outrage and a guilty appreciation of his audacity. How could a proposal so reckless, so... pragmatic, also sound so temptingly rational?

Jacqui eyed Noah carefully, her gaze sweeping

over his disheveled jeans and the way his hair fell just a bit too long, brushing against a collar that needed a good wash. His face, unshaven and undoubtedly rough to the touch, was not in line with the meticulous order of her daily life. He looked like chaos personified, a walking, talking embodiment of disorder.

For a moment, she worried over her wiring. She'd even gone and inspected his work late last night. All of the wires were neatly organized and labeled where they had been a frayed mess weeks before. The man made no sense to her orderly brain.

And here he was, offering a solution that was undeniably perfect on paper. Marry him, delay the payment, and secure her inheritance—all while keeping her business afloat. It was a lifeline, one she desperately needed. But at what cost?

"I won't come cheap," Noah said as he stood there in discount jeans and scuffed boots that looked Army-issued.

She noticed how close she was standing to him. When had he come around her desk? Where he was standing, he could dip his head and be within kissing distance. Not that she wanted that.

Jacqui took a step back, but there wasn't anywhere she could go. Her office, usually a sanctuary of organized papers and neatly lined books, felt suddenly too small, the walls inching closer as she considered the implications. Noah and she were like mixing gas and oil. Sure, together they might run an engine, but at the risk of a spectacular combustion.

"I want room and board, meaning I'll stay with you at your house. And you'll feed me. All that, plus the repairs—including work for your sister's place, in exchange for three months of marriage."

Jacqui nearly missed the edge of the chair as she sat down. She took a moment to right herself, running a hand through her hair, pressing her fingers into her throat, and taking a long, slow, deep breath. Meanwhile, Noah watched her with those piercing eyes, waiting for a reaction. Was it confidence she saw in him, or was it a challenge?

"I'm not cooking meals for you."

"You do it for everyone else in this town and the strangers that come through to visit. Why not for your dear husband?" He grinned, coming to take a seat opposite her. He crossed those thick thighs and stretched his booted feet out. They were so long they reached around to the other side of the desk.

Jacquie rolled her chair to the opposite side of the desk. "Fine, you can eat here for free."

He grinned, like he'd just won.

"And if it's three months, you'll include the light fixtures."

"Already factored into the current bid."

"They are?"

"Of course. It was a hazard. You could've gotten hurt."

Jacqui swallowed. She saw Noah's nostrils flare as his gaze fixed on her throat. She had the distinct feeling that she was letting a wolf into her home.

"So what do you say, Ms. Chou?" He leaned toward her over the desk. "Will you marry me?"

She was a warm-blooded woman. Though she hadn't day-dreamed about her own wedding or proposal, she'd seen her fair share of chick flicks. There was no rousing score accompanying Noah's proposal, but her heart still skipped a beat, her eyes prickled with a hint of moisture, and her fingers trembled—especially those on the left hand.

"I'm going to need this in writing," she finally managed to say.

Jacqui knew that engaging with Noah wouldn't be as simple as signing a contract. This was a man who would push her, possibly infuriate her, and dare her to step outside the carefully drawn lines of her life.

She took out a legal pad. "Three months, and we do this my way. Structured, planned... and temporary."

"Structured and planned."

It must have been the scratch of her pen that let her not notice he left off the word *temporary*. "You stay with me for free, eat at the restaurant for free, finish the job and anything else that might come up around it."

Noah held out his hand. "I do."

Jacqui stared at the massive paw. It would swallow her whole if she let it. She had no intention of letting it.

She took his hand, gripping hard to show him that fact. Noah grinned at the grip, as though she was a fly he could swat away. But instead of swatting, he brought her hand to his mouth and kissed her knuckles.

"What's this?" Nãinai's voice sliced through the thick tension in the room, her eyes narrowing at the sight of their joined hands.

Jacqui tried to withdraw. Noah's grip tightened.

"I asked her to marry me," he declared with a surprising gentleness that didn't match his rugged exterior.

Nãinai's eyes flicked between them, her suspicion palpable. "You just started working here."

"I did," Noah replied smoothly, his gaze never leaving Jacqui's. "It was love at first sight for me."

The words hung heavily in the air, charged with a daring. Jacqui didn't disagree. She was getting everything she wanted for just three months of pain. She'd managed worse.

Nãinai turned her scrutinizing gaze back to Jacqui. "What did she say?"

"She's sitting right here," said Jacqui.

"At first she said no," said Noah. "But I think it was out of defiance of you. Now she's saying it's too soon. What do you think, Mrs. Chou?"

"I think you should call me Nãinai."

Noah turned to her grandmother. The two of them grinned at each other. Jacqui felt like she was caught in a trap. Noah still hadn't let go of her hand. She got the sense that even after the deal was done, he would keep a piece of her. If he let her go at all.

Her grandmother's eyes darted to the legal pad on the desk, where the terms of their agreement were hastily scribbled—proof of the business deal beneath the romantic façade. In a swift move, Jacqui slid off her chair and sat down on the legal pad, concealing it beneath her. She was playing a dangerous game, but she wasn't ready to throw in her hand.

Pulling Noah toward her, Jacqui initiated a kiss meant to seal their pretense in front of her grandmother's prying eyes. The kiss was meant to be innocent, a mere performance. But as Noah responded, pulling her closer, the kiss deepened, warmth spreading through her, tangling her thoughts and senses. His lips moved against hers with an insistence that sparked a fluttering in her stomach, stirring feelings she hadn't anticipated.

What has she gotten herself into?

The question whirled through her. It scrambled her mind as Noah's hands settled on her waist. It fried her brain as he drew her even closer and sipped deeply from her parted lips.

This was supposed to be a simple agreement, a mutual benefit. Yet as they kissed, pretending for the world—or at least for Nãinai—it felt dangerously close to something neither contract nor pretense could define. As they finally broke apart, Jacqui was left breathless. But the ruse was done. Her grandmother's eyes were wide with approval and triumph. The look in Nãinai eyes said, *One down, two to go.*

CHAPTER ELEVEN

"*I*'ll see you in court!"

Noah held up his hands in front of him. It was the universal sign of surrender. Though he wasn't sure if he was trying to show that he meant no harm or if he was trying to protect himself. She looked pretty upset.

"Objection, your honor!"

"What?" Noah crossed his arms over his chest. "I just asked if you wanted a cracker."

"*His* name is not Polly. It's sexist to think all parrots are girls." This came from the woman sitting behind the massive oak desk. Like her avian friend, her feathers were clearly ruffled. Both bird and woman glared at Noah with dark eyes. Like the bird and his beak, the woman's lips pursed, like she, too, wanted to take out a chunk of him.

On the other side of the massive desk came a heavy sigh. Jacqui looked over at Noah as though he were a child acting up at the zoo. Then her annoyance shifted, and she looked past him, cocking her head just liked the bird did. She gave a bright, apologetic smile.

Noah's feet moved toward her, wanting to scoop her up into the nest of his arms. Wanting to peck at her mouth, at her ear, and her neck. Until he realized that head-cock and smile were aimed at the bird. Not at him.

"I'm sorry about him," said Jacqui.

"Consider it null and void," screeched the parrot, whose name Noah still didn't know. He cast a glare over at the bird. It puffed up its green feathers and glared back.

"Can we get back to business?" asked the bird's owner and the woman they were here to see. "You're paying by the hour."

Noah took his seat, his gaze immediately drawn to the eclectic array of bird-themed decorations that filled the office. From delicate sculptures of sparrows to vibrant paintings of exotic parrots.

Birdy was a sprightly woman with sharp eyes

that missed nothing. Her desk was cluttered with files and papers like a nest. Noah continued to scan the room, his interest piqued by a particularly intricate sculpture of an eagle in mid-flight positioned on a shelf behind Birdy. The woman was taking this nickname to an extreme. Or maybe it was her obsession with birds that had come first, and then the nickname?

"Jacqui, given your assets and the restaurant, you'll want to ensure that everything is squared away in your favor should there be any… unforeseen circumstances in the future."

Jacqui nodded, her expression serious. "The prenup needs to state that my property, including the restaurant and my home, remain with me, no matter what."

"I have no interest in running a restaurant," said Noah.

The two women turned to him, both cocking their heads. Jacqui cocked hers to the left as she regarded him; Birdy cocked hers to the right and studied him. Noah got the sense that neither woman believed his assertion.

"Still, we'll need to make sure that's all spelled out legally," said Birdy, flipping open a folder.

When Jacqui had insisted they see her lawyer,

Noah hadn't balked. Mainly because it meant he'd get to spend more time with her. Also because it reconfirmed that he was marrying a woman with brains. It made his chest puff up that his wife-to-be would make sure to protect herself from him.

Not that she had to. Noah planned to do all the protecting in this relationship. Not just with the repairs. He had a plan to build something new with Jacqui.

"I'm happy to sign whatever document will make my wife comfortable."

"I'm not your wife."

"Not yet."

Noah's words weren't a threat. However, Jacqui jerked back like she'd been struck.

"I should advise you again, Mr. Henry, that you can have your own counsel," said Birdy.

Jacqui glared at her.

Birdy shrugged.

"No need, and call me Noah. What's Jacqui's is hers. What's mine is ours."

"I'm not interested in your tools," said Jacqui.

"Objection, your honor," screeched the parrot.

Birdy snorted and then cleared her throat. "As for debt liabilities, we need to document any pre-existing debts and ensure they remain individually managed. Noah, this applies to any debts you might bring into the marriage as well."

"I don't have any debt."

"Can you prove that?" Jacqui asked suspiciously.

"How can you prove something doesn't exist?"

Jacqui opened her mouth. And then closed it.

"I don't have any line of credit or credit cards. I pay in cash. The only credit I've extended is to you."

Jacqui opened her mouth and closed it again.

"Sign on the dotted line," said the parrot from its perch.

"What about future earnings and investments made during the marriage?" said Birdy.

Noah shrugged. "I'm only interested in collecting what's owed."

His gaze dipped to Jacqui's mouth. He knew she caught the glance because of her intake of breath. It wasn't part of his plan to glance at her mouth, but he couldn't help himself. That upper lip had been so stiff since they'd met in the parking lot this afternoon and walked into this building. He wanted to kiss it into pliability.

Instead, his hands rested lightly on the stack of papers that defined the terms of their prenup. The office was quiet, save for the occasional rustle of papers and the soft hum of the air conditioning.

Only Birdy and her bird shifted on their respective perches. Both eyed Noah and Jacqui with interest.

Jacqui's expression, however, held a trace of frustration. Her brow furrowed as she glanced between Noah and the documents. "Hold on," she said, stopping Noah's hand as he reached for the pen. "You have an opportunity here. You could take advantage of me."

It took everything in Noah to hold his tongue from saying the thing he shouldn't. He wanted to take Jacqui, all right. But more than anything, he wanted her to give herself to him.

He knew she wouldn't. She wasn't yet capable of it. Because she didn't trust him. Because she didn't trust herself.

If Noah thought the rewiring job of Chow Town was an undertaking, taking on the restaurant's chef was going to be the job of his life. Just the thought of getting Jacqui Chou's wiring crossed sent a thrill through him. He had every intention of testing each and every one of her fuses to see which would make her light up, which would make her settle down. He just had to get her to open up her fuse box to him first.

"You've already denied me the only thing I asked for, Jacqui," he said, his voice low and steady.

"And what was that?"

"You said you wouldn't cook for me," Noah reminded her gently, a hint of teasing in his tone.

"I said you could eat at the restaurant for free, didn't I?"

Noah didn't answer. Instead, he signed on the dotted line. Then he turned and handed the pen to Jacqui.

She stared down at the proffered writing utensil. Slowly, she stretched out her hand. Then flexed her fingers. It was clear to Noah she was trying to avoid his touch.

He flipped the pen over, offering her the capped top while he held on to the ballpoint tip. When Jacqui's fingers seized the pen, he didn't let go immediately. Her gaze rose to his, and he saw it—that spark.

"Your witness, prosecutor," the parrot hollered.

Birdy cleared her throat. "Should I give you two a moment?"

"No, it's fine," Jacqui said, snatching the pen out of Noah's hold and signing her name beside his.

Noah felt a quiet resolution settle over them. The prenup defined their financial boundaries. But he had every intention of rerouting the unwritten romantic grid of their marriage.

CHAPTER TWELVE

*J*acqui stared at her reflection and didn't wholly recognize herself. The mirror showed a woman transformed, her hair artfully arranged in swirls and curls, with delicate flowers woven through like whispers of spring. Bunny and Jules had insisted on the floral accents. Despite her initial resistance, Jacqui now found herself grateful for their persistence.

She hadn't planned to tell anybody what was happening today. She could still barely believe it herself. But she'd never been able to keep anything from her best friend. And once Bunny knew, she insisted Jacqui tell her sisters.

"You're doing this because of Nãinai, aren't you?"

Jules continued to add flowers to Jacqui's hair.

Her baby sister had always had an artful touch, which was why her cakes and cookies were so sought after. People loved to look at them as much as they loved to eat them.

Jacqui herself looked edible now with the soft petals adding a touch of whimsy to her elegant updo. Jules' design framed her face with gentle bursts of color that seemed to echo her blooming feelings. It was a contrast to her usual pragmatic self, confined within the walls of Chow Town. Today, however, she was not just a restaurateur but a bride. She wasn't in the back of the house, overseeing her family's recipes. She was the topper on the wedding cake.

"Since when have you known your sister to bow to grannie-pressure?" Bunny stepped in, adjusting one of Jacqui's stubborn curls.

Jacqui was grateful for her friend's save. She was so lightheaded from the pins in her hair and the floral scents wafting up her nose that she just might have told her sister the truth.

Jules frowned and then raised a brow. "Fair point. But they've only known each other a week."

"Ten days," said Jacqui.

"You just never said—"

"She said something to me," said Bunny.

Jules' face fell, her fingers hesitating on the

flower she had been placing in Jacqui's hair. "You didn't think you could tell me that you were falling in love, Jacks?"

Jacqui swallowed. Lying didn't come easy to her. Leaving bits and bobs out or telling half-truths she could manage. But an outright lie?

"We didn't fall in love."

Jules gasped. Her hands fell to her sides. The last flower fluttered to the ground like it was fainting.

Bunny scrunched her nose. Her brows drew together in a wince. Her gaze said, *I can't help you now.*

"It was a practical decision," Jacqui insisted.

"This *is* because of Nāinai." Jules' voice was almost a whine, like when Jacqui told her she couldn't have any more sweets for the day.

"That's a bonus. I won't lie. But Noah, he's...steady."

"Steady?"

Jacqui struggled for the words to calm her sister's worries. Then she realized they were right there at the tip of her brain. "You ever met someone who makes you feel safe? Noah's honest, even to his own detriment. He's strong and capable. When I'm with him, I just feel like I can take a break and not worry, you know?"

"Yeah, I know. It's how I've felt my whole life with you as my big sister."

Jacqui opened her arms, and Jules came into them. As she squeezed her, Jacqui wondered if her baby sister had lost a bit of weight. She felt just a touch too thin. She'd have to cart lunch over to her for the next couple of days and sit with her while she ate to be sure she was keeping up her caloric intake.

"Except the parts where you hover over me." Jules' voice was muffled as she her face was turned into Jacqui's bosom.

Jacqui gave one last squeeze before she let her baby sister go.

"I have to go make sure my phone is charged so I can stream it to Jami," said Jules.

"Just keep her on mute," said Jacqui.

"Right. I love you, Jacqui-Bear."

"Love you too, Jule-bug."

Once Jules left the room, Jacqui winced. She knew it was coming. And come it did. Bunny rounded on her.

"Spill it."

"Spill what?"

"I know you were with my sister the other day. With your husband-to-be. Birdy wouldn't talk. Something about client confidentiality. Which means you're her client. What are you three cooking up?"

Jacqui could keep things from her sisters, but she couldn't keep anything from Bunny. The two of them were a couple of peas in a pod. Bunny was also the eldest sister. She'd understand.

"It's just temporary so—"

"So that you'll get your inheritance."

Jacqui nodded.

Bunny cursed under her breath. "So you signed a prenup? Is that why you were at Birdy's?"

Jacqui nodded.

"Okay, at least you're being smart about this insanity. But are you sure? About him?"

Jacqui's thoughts drifted to Noah. The memory of their conversation in Birdy's office came back to her, clear and poignant. His words had touched something deep within her, revealing layers of connection and care she hadn't dared to acknowlededge until that moment. He hadn't wanted anything from her. She'd never experienced that before. Except with Bunny.

"It's going to be all right. If not, Birdy will rake him over the coals and then hand him off to you."

That seemed to satisfy her best friend. "All right,

but if you need an out, you give me a signal, and I'll object so loud and fast it'll make his head spin."

"I love you."

"Love you, too. You insane woman."

"I'm getting married."

"You look beautiful."

Jacqui looked at herself in the mirror again. She did look beautiful. She wondered what Noah would think. Then she immediately shut that kind of thinking down.

A gentle knock on the door pulled her from her reverie. "Jacqui, are you ready?" Jules' voice, tinged with excitement, filtered through the door.

As Jacqui stepped through the softly lit corridor leading to the small, flower-adorned arch where Noah waited, her mind wandered back to the days of her childhood, to the love she had observed between her parents. It had been a gentle, steadfast sort of love, one that filled the corners of her childhood home with laughter and warmth. Her father's eyes would light up whenever her mother walked into the room, and her mother's laughter was a frequent, comforting sound that echoed through the hallways.

That warmth had dimmed far too soon, extinguished by a sudden, tragic twist of fate when her mother passed away from an aggressive form of cancer. The shock had barely worn off when, less than a year later, her father followed, his heart seemingly unable to bear the weight of his grief. Jacqui had always believed he'd held on just long enough to ensure she was old enough to take custody of Jules and Jami, to keep them together as a family.

The losses had seeded a deep wariness about love in Jacqui's heart. To her, love was a dangerous, debilitating force that could tear you apart from the inside, leaving nothing but sorrow in its wake. This wariness had shaped her into a woman who viewed relationships as transactions, safeguards against loneliness rather than genuine emotional connections. Today, her impending marriage to Noah was framed in her mind as a strategic move for financial stability, not a leap of faith in love.

As she approached the sun-drenched patio where the ceremony was set, her thoughts were interrupted by her first glimpse of Noah waiting for her. He was clad in his military uniform. The white suit highlighted the broad set of his shoulders and the quiet strength that emanated from his stance. Seeing him like this—so handsome, so ready, so hers—made her heart perform a traitorous leap. For a moment,

Jacqui's carefully constructed defenses wavered, and warmth seeped through the cracks of her guarded heart.

CHAPTER THIRTEEN

*N*oah stood at the altar, his best man Fish beside him, both decked out in their dress whites that fit slightly tighter after these last couple of years. Neither man had grown a dad bod. Instead, civilian life seemed to have made them bigger. Probably all that sleep they were getting these days. There was something to be said about rest days in the adrenaline and exercise cycles.

The town church was quaint. Beams of sunlight streamed through the stained glass windows. The beams cast colorful patterns on the polished wooden pews where their closest friends and family sat. Well, Jacqui's closest friends and family. Noah only knew one soul in here.

"You sure about this, man?" Fish asked as he tugged at his collar, eying the cross on the wall.

Fish had left the church years ago. That exodus had happened in the theater of war. Some service members clung to their faith after picking up arms. Others turned away from it after seeing the worst of humanity.

The minister, an elderly man with a keen, observant gaze, slid his attention over to Noah, waiting for the answer alongside Noah's only friend in the space. It wasn't the first once-over the man of the cloth had given to Noah.

It was as though the minister could sense the lie that Noah was telling. Actually, no. Not the lie. It was as though the minister could sense the truth Noah wasn't telling: that this marriage was going to be real for him despite the temporary stamp his fake fiancée was planning.

Noah shot Fish a glare that could have frozen the ocean, his expression enough to quiet any further commentary from his friend. Then Noah turned to the minister, his smile broadening. "I've never been more sure of anything in my life."

No truer words had ever been spoken. The minister's nod felt like a blessing, a benediction. Even though this wasn't a Catholic church. Even though Noah hadn't been inside of a church... likely since his baptism.

Didn't matter. Both he and the man of God knew he spoke the truth.

He did want this—more than he had ever wanted anything. He wanted to marry Jacqui, to be there to hold her hand through every challenge, to have the right to stand by her side not just today, but every day after.

He wanted to fight with her and see that spark. Then he wanted to taste the fire inside of her. It would be such a good burn.

"It's been two weeks," Fish continued, oblivious to the miracle happening within his friend. "I didn't even think you liked her. No one likes her."

Noah shot Fish a backhand against his chest. "That's my wife you're talking about."

Fish coughed and rubbed at his chest. "Are you sure she's not blackmailing you?"

Noah forced a laugh for the minister's benefit. "Do you think she could make a big man like me do what she wanted?"

Fish didn't even hesitate. "Yes."

Noah considered that, then canted his head. Yeah, it was accurate. His Jacqui could make him do just about anything with a curl of her lip.

His Jacqui. He liked the sound of it. Pretty soon, he'd have the right to say it out loud.

The doors at the back of the church opened, and there she was. Jacqui stood framed in the doorway, bathed in the soft glow of the afternoon sun, looking so breathtakingly beautiful that Noah almost swallowed his tongue from want. Her dress was simple yet elegant, accentuating her figure gracefully, her hair adorned with flowers that seemed to have been picked just for this moment.

For a split second, everything else faded—the guests, the church, even the minister. There was only Jacqui, her presence pulling him like a tide. Noah felt a powerful urge to close the distance between them, to start their future together with a sprint rather than a walk. He almost stepped forward, nearly forgetting the protocol of the moment.

Out of the corner of his eye, Noah noticed the minister's stern expression soften into a smile of approval, his eyes twinkling with amusement. It was clear to anyone watching that here stood a man hopelessly, irrevocably in love. The only person who didn't see it, who couldn't see it, was the bride-to-be.

Jacqui walked down the aisle toward him, each step measured and stiff. She looked like a wild animal that would spook if touched the wrong way.

Noah kept his hands behind his back. The sound of the organ swelled in a beautiful crescendo, echoing the racing of his heartbeat.

When she finally reached him, Noah unclenched his hands and held out his open palm. There was a moment where he wasn't sure if she'd take it.

She looked at his offering. Her jaw ticked. Her chest rose and fell with a deep intake of breath. And then, finally, she laid her fingertips in the palm of his hand.

Noah felt a surge of completeness, a sense that everything that had led him to this point—every decision, every doubt, every turn in his road—had been right.

"Dearly beloved, we are gathered here today in the presence of these witnesses to join Noah and Jacqui in matrimony."

Noah's hands were clasped with Jacqui's, his palms slightly sweaty as he squeezed her fingers reassuringly. He felt the steady thrum of his heart, a rhythm that echoed through the very foundations of the church.

"Noah, do you take Jacqui to be your lawfully wedded wife, to live together in holy matrimony, to love her, comfort her, honor, and keep her, in sickness and in health, forsaking all others, for as long as you both shall live?"

"I do," he declared, each of the two words resonating like a solemn oath sworn rather than a mere vow given. It felt as though with each syllable, he was binding his life to hers, committing to a shared future filled with unknowns yet anchored by this moment of unity.

As the minister turned to Jacqui, Noah watched her, his eyes locked on hers, searching for a sign of genuine emotion. "And do you, Jacqui, take Noah to be your lawfully wedded husband, to live together in holy matrimony, to love him, comfort him, honor, and keep him, in sickness and in health, forsaking all others, for as long as you both shall live?"

"I do."

Jacqui's response was clear and confident, her voice carrying through the church. Her eyes held his, and in them, he saw not just the brilliant business-woman he respected but a woman who might indeed come to love him, as he was already sure he loved her.

Their hands squeezed slightly, a tangible connection amidst the vows, reinforcing their bond as they turned to face their future together. The reverend's final blessing echoed around them, sealing their commitment as they prepared to step forward into a new life that was now theirs to define.

"You may now kiss the bride."

"Wait? What?"

The reverend turned to Jacqui. "I said you may now kiss your husband, my dear."

"Right now? In front of everybody?"

"Since when are you shy?" came Nãinai's voice from the front pew.

Jacqui looked to Noah in a panic. First his eyes, then his mouth. Then at some spot on his shoulder, as though she couldn't handle even the sight of his lips.

Noah maneuvered them until he had his back to everyone, blocking out her family and friends from sight of what he was about to do. Only the minister, Fish, and Jacqui's sister, could see Noah move in on his wife.

His wife. Jacqui was now his wife. The knowledge of it sent his blood racing. Unfortunately, all he saw was panic in her eyes.

"Tell me what you want to do," Noah whispered, caring only for her comfort.

"I… I suppose we have to."

"We don't have to do anything you don't want to."

"We don't?"

"Hmm." Noah shook his head, speaking low and gentle. "It's entirely up to you. I'll do whatever you want."

Jacqui's hand came to rest on his chest as she gazed up into his eyes.

"Do you want me to kiss you here, Jacqui? In front of all of these people? Or do you want to wait until we get home?"

That snapped her out of it. Jacqui glared. But she must have realized she couldn't say anything cutting. So she rose up on her tiptoes and pressed a quick peck to his cheek.

"There. You all satisfied?"

"We're all fine," called Nāinai. "But I don't think your husband is."

Nāinai was both right and wrong. Noah had gotten a taste of his wife. When he got her alone, he'd gorge himself on the full meal.

Soon.

CHAPTER FOURTEEN

*S*he'd asked them not to do this. It was the first time Jacqui's staff had disobeyed her. There was nothing she could do to retaliate. Not when a good portion of the town was watching.

The reception at Chow Town was in full swing. Strings of lights twinkled from the ceiling, casting a warm, inviting glow over the assembled guests. The air was alive with the sound of laughter, clinking glasses, and the soft strains of music that filled the space between conversations. Jacqui stood near the entrance, watching as her employees and friends clapped Noah on the back, welcoming him into their close-knit community with hearty embraces and cheerful toasts.

She glared at the scene, feeling like she was back

in culinary school all over again. One of those times when she'd prepped a protein or sauce that was stellar only to have the head chef, always a male, get the credit for the finished dish.

Today at her wedding, she'd been there, too. She'd been at the altar with Noah. She'd said those same solemn vows. Why was he getting all of the claps on the back and congratulations?

Possibly because she was in a corner near the entrance while everyone else was at the center of the restaurant. Meanwhile, Noah grinned and greeted her people like he had just won the high school homecoming game and kissed the cheerleader. That would make her the cheerleader.

Jacqui brought her fingers to her lips, brushing them lightly across the surface where his kiss still lingered. It had been just a quick peck, a soft brush of lips that marked their union. Yet somehow the sensation had imprinted itself in her memory, stubbornly refusing to fade.

As a chef, Jacqui had always been obsessed with flavors, with identifying and understanding each component that danced on her palate. Noah's kiss, brief as it was, had left a complex taste that she couldn't quite decipher. Her mind wandered through the possibilities.

There was a hint of herbs, perhaps basil, one of her favorites, which she often added to her water bottle along with a slice of cucumber. Then there was the spice, like cayenne, sharp and thrilling, hinting at depths to his personality she was only just beginning to explore. Underlying it all, there was something unexpectedly sweet, a note of warmth that suggested caramel or honey, which softened the sharper edges of the spice and herb.

This combination, much like Noah himself, was unexpected—a blend of strength and warmth, spice and sweetness. It was a flavor profile that was entirely unique to him, reflecting his complex nature and the life he'd led before they'd come together. As Jacqui stood there, analyzing the remnants of their kiss, she realized she was more than curious—she was captivated.

She was also captured.

Noah caught her eye from across the room, a knowing smile curling his lips as if he could sense her thoughts. She turned away. But turning away from him made her remember the maneuver he'd used when they'd been on display.

Tell me what you want.

No one ever asked her that. Aside from Bunny.

But Jacqui hadn't felt the tug of war to kiss Bunny at the same time as she wanted to punch her.

It had felt good to be blocked from everyone else's sight. It had felt good to have him take the decision away from her. That one or two moments had been the vacation she'd needed over these last years of responsibility. And now it was gone.

"Ready to go home?" Noah asked, his voice a gentle hum over the buzz of the remaining guests.

Jacqui's heart did a little skip. *Home.* The word felt both foreign and incredibly right. She hadn't forgotten this part of their deal. She'd planned for it. So she nodded, swallowing the lump that had suddenly formed in her throat.

"We'll see you next week, boss," Nia called out, raising her wineglass in a half salute.

Jacqui scoffed, her business-owner instincts kicking in despite the day's emotions. "I'll be back at work in the morning, on time."

An awkward silence fell over the small group that had gathered around. Smiles faltered. Eyes darted between Noah and Jacqui. Everyone was suddenly unsure how to react.

They knew Jacqui well—her dedication, her tireless work ethic. But this was her wedding night. A buzz went around the room as though they all were trying to decide if she was joking or not.

As if on cue, the tension broke. One by one, their faces cracked into knowing smiles, the earlier hesitation dissolving into amused chuckles. Jacqui, puzzled, turned just in time to catch Noah shaking his head at her with a broad grin, clearly indicating that she would not, in fact, be back to work in the morning.

Jacqui's eyes widened in outrage, but no one saw. Noah wrapped an arm around her shoulders, pulling her close, as any newlywed husband might do to his new bride. She was married. She was taking her new husband home.

She knew the parameters of the restaurant. She had the prenup. But what were they going to do in her house? For three months?

As Jacqui settled into the passenger seat of Noah's truck, the contrast between the tidiness of her own car and the chaos inside his struck her immediately. Maps were haphazardly folded and stuffed into the side door pockets, various camping gear was piled in the back seat, and an assortment of snack wrappers and coffee cups adorned the cup holders and floorboards. The air was a mix of pine air freshener battling against the earthy scent of dirt and firewood—a clear testament to his recent outdoor adventures.

"Your truck looks like a pigsty." Jacqui gingerly moved a crumpled-up jacket to make more room for herself.

"Yeah, I've been mostly living out of it. Camping a lot. Haven't really lived in a house since I left my parents' place to join the military. It's been bases, hotels, or the great outdoors ever since."

"Sounds lonely."

So was her house, since her sisters had struck out on their own. Jules lived in an apartment across town. Jami was traveling the world, living out of a suitcase.

"I like the freedom, and the stars are more friendly than any ceiling I've known."

The truck's headlights cut through the darkness of the night, casting long shadows on the road ahead. Inside the cab, the soft glow of the dashboard illuminated Noah's profile, highlighting the lines of his face, the curve of his jaw, and the slight furrow of his brow as he concentrated on the road.

Moments later, his truck came to a gentle halt in the driveway of Jacqui's neatly kept home. He cut the engine, and the quiet of the evening wrapped around them like a soft shawl. Jacqui reached for the door handle, ready to escape into the familiar sanctuary of her house.

Noah's voice stopped her. "Wait."

Curious, Jacqui paused, watching as Noah quickly climbed out of the truck and moved around to her side. The crisp night air whispered through the trees, rustling the leaves in a soothing rhythm. Under the soft glow of the porch light, Noah opened the passenger door with a gallant flourish.

Deciding to play along with whatever he had in mind, Jacqui extended her hand to him, expecting perhaps a gentle guide out of the truck. Instead, Noah took her hand and then used his other to lift her from her seat and into his arms.

"What are you doing?" Jacqui demanded as her feet dangled above the ground.

"It's tradition. The husband is supposed to carry the wife over the threshold. It's good luck."

"I'm heavy," she warned, half-expecting him to set her down.

Noah just shrugged, adjusting his hold on her. "I work out. And I can bench press a lot more than you think."

Indignant and a bit embarrassed by being carried so effortlessly, Jacqui squirmed in his arms, attempting to climb down. "Put me down, Noah. I can walk."

As she wriggled, Noah winced slightly, his expression flickering with a brief flash of pain.

Jacqui immediately stilled, her concern flaring. "Did I hurt you?"

"No, no," he assured her quickly, though she noticed him adjust his grip slightly. "Just caught me off guard."

Jacqui relaxed slightly, allowing him to carry her up the steps to the front door. She was constantly on her feet. Constantly chasing after people or watching over their shoulders. Now her view was over Noah's shoulder. Her feet were blessedly weightless. She should not like this.

But she did. She felt as if something was unlocking inside of her.

"Key?"

Jacqui stared at him. At his lips. Then his eyes.

Noah lifted a brow.

"Oh. Key." She produced the house key from her purse and handed it to him.

Noah shifted her weight again. This time, she didn't protest. He unlocked the door, and they were inside. They were inside alone.

"You can put me down now."

Noah glanced at her. For a moment, she wasn't sure if he was going to let her go. She wasn't sure if she wanted him to. But he did.

When Jacqui's feet touched down, all of the weight returned to her shoulders. The events of the day came crashing down around her. She needed a moment to compose herself. No, she needed all night to set herself to rights again. She couldn't let him see her not at her best, so she made a quick dash for the stairs.

"Am I supposed to follow you?"

"Nope. There's the guest room." She pointed off to the side. "Help yourself to whatever's in the fridge. Good night, Noah."

Once she hit the last stair, she took off running to her room. Once behind the closed door, Jacqui pressed her back to the wood. It didn't relieve any of the weight. She slid down to the floor and knocked her head back against the door a couple of times. It was the first time in a long time that she didn't feel entirely in control.

CHAPTER FIFTEEN

He'd slept in worse conditions.

Noah stood surveying the guest room of Jacqui's house, his duffle bag slung over his shoulder. The room was neat and cozy, decorated in soft pastels that reminded him of a spring day. The walls were painted a gentle lavender, and the curtains that fluttered slightly from the open window were a pale, airy pink, filtering the moonlight in.

A dresser bore porcelain figurines and framed photographs of people he didn't recognize, each smiling from within silver and ceramic frames. A fluffy white rug lay on the floor. He sensed the softness under his boots. It was a contrast to the hard, utilitarian surfaces he was accustomed to in military barracks or the gritty, unyielding sands of desert outposts.

It was disorienting, this gentle, feminine room. But what disturbed him most was the bed. The single bed, pushed up against one wall, was draped with a quilt made up of a thousand different pink and periwinkle squares. Plump pillows were piled at the head, their cases edged in delicate lace.

Noah dropped his bag onto the bed. The springs gasped like a lady about to faint. There was no way that dainty bed would hold his weight. The way the mattress sagged under just his bag didn't inspire confidence. He was a solidly built guy, and the idea of spending a night on that precarious setup was less than appealing.

An idea sparked in his mind, mischievous and potentially very convenient. If the guest bed was out of commission, well, he'd have no choice but to share the master bedroom with Jacqui.

He took a step back, gauging the distance with the eye of a man who had jumped from more than a few high places in his time. Then, with a quick sprint, he leaped onto the bed.

The impact was more than the poor bed could handle. There was a moment of eerie silence as the structure bore his weight. Noah frowned in disappointment at the bed's efforts to hold him up. The frame's efforts were short-lived, though.

With a dramatic snap, it gave way. Noah went down with it, a tangle of limbs and broken slats. The mattress hit the floor with a thud that was surely heard throughout the house.

The sound of the crash was oddly satisfying. The chaos of splintered wood and twisted metal were a clear sign of mission accomplished. However, the feeling of the crash was another story; it definitely hurt more than he had anticipated.

Almost immediately, he heard the rapid patter of footsteps approaching. Jacqui burst into the room, her eyes wide with alarm. He saw the sparks in the dim light of the room, and it heated the places where he was hurt.

"Noah?" Jacqui rushed to his side amidst the wreckage. Her hands fluttered over him, gentle and quick, as she checked him for injuries. "Are you okay?"

"I'm not sure," Noah groaned, exaggerating his discomfort as he caught her concerned look. The truth was, the fall had hurt, but the pain was nothing compared to the warmth spreading through him at her touch.

The frame twisted awkwardly beneath him like a

failed circuit. He groaned, the sound echoing slightly in the small room, not entirely feigned as the jolt from the crash had genuinely rattled his bones.

"Where does it hurt?"

"Just here... Everywhere."

Her hands were careful as they moved to his legs, her fingers pressing lightly against his chest and his back, searching for any sign of real injury. Noah didn't hold back his groan. Too bad it sounded more like pleasure.

The touch of her fingers was like a jolt, far different from the pain of the fall coursing through him. It was as if her touch was reestablishing connections along frayed wires within him, each contact sparking pathways long dormant.

There was a delicate scent of vanilla that clung to her, mingling with the sharper tang of worry that filled the air. He watched her, her face so close to his, her eyes focused intently on him. It was intimate, this concerned scrutiny, and it made his heart beat faster.

"I'm fine. I'm made of strong stock. I'll just sleep it off and be right as rain in the morning."

"Are you sure?"

"Absolutely sure."

It was a gamble. Every move with her had to be.

With a woman like Jacqui, Noah knew he had to make every idea appear to be her own.

"All right," she said. "I'll go and make up the couch."

Noah's feigned grimace fell into utter disbelief. "The couch?"

"The other two bedrooms are empty since my sisters moved out. No beds."

No beds. Meaning there was only one other bed in the house: the one in Jacqui's bedroom. Noah's sole mission was to get into that bed.

"I don't know about the couch," he hedged, lacing a groan into his voice. "I think I need a mattress after that fall."

"There's only one other bed in the house—mine."

"I'll take yours."

"You're kicking me out of my bed?"

"Of course not. It's a big bed, isn't it? We can share."

"No we can't."

Noah groaned again. He wobbled as he climbed to his feet. Then he limped, placing his hand on his back. "Fine, I'll take the couch."

He walked stiffly, playing it up. As he walked, each step was careful and measured, his body held rigidly, as if fearing that any normal movement might exacerbate his "injury." Every few steps, he would wince sharply, a visual punctuation that he was not okay, his hand pressing more firmly against his back as if to quell a surge of pain.

Noah's eyes flicked toward Jacqui, stealing quick glances under furrowed brows to gauge her reaction. Was she buying it? Did she look concerned enough to step in and offer aid, or perhaps some soothing words? He wasn't so sure. So he pulled out the big guns.

"Can't wait to walk into work tomorrow." Another limp. "What will they think you did to me when I come in bruised and limping after our wedding night?"

Jacqui pursed her lips. Then she worried the lower one with her fingers.

"I just hope this doesn't lay me up from finishing the work on Jules' bakery."

"I see what you're doing."

"I'm trying to get comfortable on your couch." Noah punched the couch cushions, trying to tenderize their firmness before lowering himself down.

Jacqui cocked her head and put her hands on her hips, glaring at him.

"What?" Noah pressed his hand to his heart,

trying to look innocent. "You think I'm going to touch you if we sleep in the same bed?"

Jacqui said nothing.

"Do you think I want to touch you?"

He saw her confidence falter then. Noah wanted to kick himself in his own butt for making her doubt his feelings for her. But first he had to make her feel comfortable enough to have feelings for him.

"Scout's honor, Jacqui, I won't touch you. Unless, of course, you ask me to."

"I'm not going to ask you to." Her voice was husky with denial.

"Then there's nothing we have to worry about."

CHAPTER SIXTEEN

*J*acqui had been a lucid dreamer all her life. Whenever her sisters woke from a nightmare, she'd tell them to simply change the dream the next time. Jami and Jules had looked at her like she was crazy when she said these things to them as kids. Jacqui hadn't learned until later that not everyone dreamed the way she did. Not everyone knew they were dreaming or could sometimes control aspects of their dreams. Some didn't dream at all.

She'd always looked up to the heroines of movies like Nancy in *Nightmare on Elm Street* who could control what happened in dreams. Granted, Jacqui didn't have many nightmares. Well, there was that one recurring dream of marathon mis en place prepping where she'd be chopping onions or turning artichokes for a sadistic chef with knife fingers. But truly, she found prep soothing. It was cooking that gave her hives these days. And she would always wake herself up if she got too close to a lit stove.

She wasn't dreaming of cooking right now. She was dreaming of sleeping. Which was an odd dream to have. She wasn't alone in this dream, just like she knew she wasn't alone in her bed. Noah was beside her.

Do you think I'm going to touch you?

He wasn't speaking. His eyes were closed, his hands behind his head. Just as he'd been when he climbed into her bed back in reality.

Do you think I want to touch you?

Jacqui wasn't so sure about that, back on the other side of her eyelids. In the dream, Noah's eyes opened. He looked straight at her with that unreadable look. Just like in reality, his gaze tracked her. There was also that smirk on his mouth. It was the smirk she couldn't read.

"Do you think I want to touch you?" he said.

"Yes," Jacqui answered. Because in the dream, she could tell him the truth. She could tell him that she wanted him to touch her.

As a lucid dreamer, Jacqui had long mastered the

art of navigating her nocturnal landscapes, aware of her dreaming state yet fully immersed in the experiences it offered. Tonight, her dream-self moved with purpose across the expanse of bed sheets that separated her from her temporary husband.

In the dream, she could look her fill at his large body. In her dream, she could inhale his spicy scent without trying to be sneaky about it. In her dream, she could touch him.

"Scout's honor, I won't touch you."

Jacqui wanted Noah to touch her. But in this dream, he wouldn't. Nothing she did seemed able to make him.

Sometimes, she couldn't control every aspect of her dreams. But she could control what *she* did. So *she* touched *him*.

Noah's chest was bare in the dream. Back in reality, he'd pulled on a T-shirt before he'd come to bed. She saw the red bruising there from the twin bed's collapse. She felt another pang of guilt for forcing him into the guest room when she knew full well his big body wouldn't fit the bed frame.

Now she ran her fingers over those bruised spots. She reached out, her fingertips barely grazing the firm expanse of his chest. The warmth of his skin beneath her touch was palpable, radiating a comforting heat that pulsed like a gentle breeze against the cool night air of the dream-meadow. The solid, rhythmic beat of his heart thumped under her touch, grounding the surrealism of the dream with something undeniably real.

Jacqui's fingers traced the outline of his pecs, each muscle defined and smooth under the softness of his skin. The texture was like silk draped over stones, a softness belying the strength that lay beneath. Moving downward, her hands encountered the ridges of his abs, each one a subtle rise and fall in the landscape of his body. They were like rows of carefully carved hillocks, shaped from years of discipline and physical work. The sensation was exhilarating—each muscle a testament to his strength yet yielding under her curious exploration.

Her senses were alight with the proximity of him. His scent was a mix of the fresh outdoors and something uniquely Noah. It was a clean, invigorating smell that wove itself into the fabric of her dream.

Jacqui leaned closer. The anticipation built. Her heart pounded louder in her chest. Her eyes locked on to his lips, observing the way the moonlight played over the contours, casting them in a soft light. She could almost taste him already—the slight hint of mint from toothpaste, perhaps, mingled with the natural flavor that she imagined was all his own. The thought made her mouth water, her lips parting slightly as she inched closer.

"Are you going to kiss me, Jacqui?"

Why hadn't she kissed him for real at the ceremony? Then she wouldn't have to be pawing at him in her dreams. That peck had done nothing but make her thirsty, like she'd had the last drop in her canteen while in the middle of the desert. Now she was looking down at a crystal blue pool of fresh water.

"You can if you want," he said. "You can kiss me. You don't need to ask my permission."

"I don't need to ask your permission. This is my dream."

There went that smirk again. "I'm in your dreams?"

"Yes. This is my dream."

The smirk widened. She didn't like that look on his face. She needed to rearrange it. She willed her mind to paint a different picture of her dream man. But that knowing grin wouldn't leave his face.

That wasn't normally how things happened in her lucid dreams. And when had his hands gone back behind his head? And when had his shirt gone back on?

Jacqui blinked. And blinked again. But she didn't wake up. Because she was already wide awake.

She looked down to find that she'd been the one to breach the barrier she'd made between them. She was the one snuggled up against him. She was the one who had touched him, was now leaning over him for a kiss.

She scrambled off the bed so fast the sheets tangled around her legs. She managed to hop free without falling flat on her face. With her feet and legs free, she dashed into the bathroom and locked the door behind her. Because she lived in there now.

CHAPTER SEVENTEEN

$\mathcal{N}$oah had barely slept all night. He'd lain awake for hours listening to the soothing sound of Jacqui breathing. Her little snores were adorable. The snorts and gurgles settled him because he knew that she rested deeply with him beside her. That kind of deep sleep only came when someone felt safe and secure.

The other soft sounds of night hummed around the edges of Noah's consciousness. His gaze rarely strayed from his bedmate. He was captivated by the rise and fall of her chest. The flutter of eyelashes against her cheeks. The way her hair spilled over the pillow like a cascade of sunlight in the dark. It grounded him, this knowledge that she rested so

SHANAE JOHNSON

deeply with him by her side, in her space, in her sanctuary.

Throughout the night, he had felt Jacqui shifting closer to him, her movements slow and languid, like the soft tide of an ocean inching its way up a sandy beach. Noah remained still each time, his body tense due to his earlier insistence on boundaries. With every unconscious advance she made, his heart raced faster, the beat echoing loud in the silence of the room.

It was her fingers that broached the divide between them. When they came to rest on his chest, Noah surrendered his heart to her. The touch burned through the fabric of his shirt, imprinting itself directly onto his skin. He kept his hands up and behind his head, not touching her as he promised. But he clutched at the white cotton of the pillow like a white flag.

Jacqui's fingers curled slightly, possessively, as if in her sleep she claimed him as hers just as much as he silently claimed her. She wanted him. Just not consciously.

That was fine. All the fun would be in making her admit the truth. So when her eyes opened hours later and she found herself flush against him, the games had begun.

"Are you going to kiss me, Jacqui? You can if you want. You don't need to ask my permission."

"I don't need to ask your permission. This is my dream."

"I'm in your dreams?"

"Yes. This is my dream."

The early morning light filtered through the curtains, casting a soft glow across the room. It was one of those rare, still moments that pressed pause on the world outside. The rising sun slowly came up like a dimmer. He could almost hear the sunbeams scrambling up the walls.

Jacqui's movements were unhurried, and that was good. Noah wanted to stay in this moment forever. She was sleep-addled and a bit confused, but she was still the most beautiful thing he'd ever seen in his life.

Her head lifted from the pillow, and the sunlight caught in her hair, turning it into a halo of golden strands that fanned out around her like rays of sun. It was as if she carried her own sunrise, a personal dawn that brightened the space around her.

Her eyes, dark and deep, opened slowly, the sleepiness still clouding them like the soft fog of early morning. Gradually, as she blinked away the remnants of dreams, her gaze cleared, becoming sharp and vivid, grounding her back in the reality of the new day. Even disheveled, with her hair tousled and her nightclothes slightly askew, she looked breathtaking—raw, real, and radiant.

Noah watched, almost holding his breath, as the transformation took place. There was an undeniable beauty in Jacqui's unguarded moments, in the honesty of her sleep-softened features and the unselfconscious way she greeted the morning. To him, she seemed more herself than ever, stripped of any façade, existing purely and simply.

She blinked a few more times, coming to realize that she was not dreaming. She scrambled off the bed, but not before Noah got a sight of toned legs and toes painted a fiery red. At that moment, he developed a foot fetish.

Seeing as she was not coming out of the bathroom anytime soon, Noah decided to take pity on his wife. He got out of bed and headed down to the guest room. He got dressed and headed into the kitchen, turning that phrase over and over in his head.

My wife. Jacqui was his wife. He'd slept next to his wife. And she'd sought his warmth in the middle of the night. She'd dreamed of his kisses. Noah was going to make his wife's dreams come true.

"What are you doing?" his wife demanded a half hour later.

"I'm trying to work your fancy toaster."

"Why?" Jacqui's voice was all suspicion and accusation.

"Because I'm making you breakfast, Mrs. Henry."

"It's Ms. Chou or Chef. And you're murdering those eggs."

Jacqui's body checked him with those curvy hips, bumping him from his place at the stove. Noah only moved because she wanted him to, not because she physically could make him. Before he relinquished pride of place, she grabbed the spatula from him. Then froze.

Noah had seen battle-scarred soldiers return to the field with that look. They'd been certain they had recovered from the horrors they'd seen and endured and were ready to do their job again. They'd been wrong.

Jacqui stood frozen with the spatula in hand. She looked down at the kitchen tool like it was a grenade. Her hand gripped the utensil so tightly that her knuckles turned white. Her eyes stared blankly at the sizzling pan, but it was clear she wasn't really seeing it.

Yeah, it was the same look he'd seen on the faces

of soldiers. The look of seeing the ravages of their wounds when they woke up in a medical tent. The look of witnessing the loss of a comrade. They would freeze up at a sound or a movement, a flood of memories paralyzing them, their faces drained of color, eyes wide and unseeing, as if they were looking at a ghost only they could see. As far as he knew, Jacqui had never seen a battlefield.

"Jacqui?" Noah's voice was gentle, laced with concern. He stepped closer, his presence cautious and non-threatening. He reached out slowly and placed his hand over hers on the spatula, easing it gently from her grasp. He kept his hand on hers.

Jacqui blinked slowly, her breath hitching as she returned to the present. She looked around, disoriented for a moment, before her gaze settled on Noah. The vulnerability in her eyes was raw, her usual composure stripped away by the grip of a silent battle Noah could only guess at. Then, in another blink, it was gone.

She snatched her hand away from his. "I told you you could eat at the restaurant. I'm not cooking for you."

"I was cooking for you."

She swallowed as though she didn't understand

his words. Then bobbed her head in acceptance. But that was short-lived.

Jacqui shook her head in a clear sign of rejection of the notion of being taken care of. "I don't have time for this. I have to get to the farmer's market for produce."

"I'll pack breakfast up."

"Why?" She looked like a flustered hen.

"I'm coming with you."

"Why?"

He didn't bother answering. He searched out Tupperware and put the put the eggs and barely brown toast inside the plastic's belly.

"Noah, about last night..." Jacqui began, her voice hesitating slightly. "I... I need to apologize for invading your space in the bed. I thought..."

She tried to swallow again. The lump in her throat was nearly visible. Noah wanted to trace his fingers over the spot. He wanted to press his mouth there to soothe away any discomfort. He took a step toward her.

Jacqui stepped back. In a blink of her eyes, the hesitation and vulnerability were gone. So was the lump. "I thought you were my ex. That's why I cuddled up to you. It won't happen again."

Noah felt a sharp sting of emotion. His hands

balled into fists, draining all the blood from his fingertips. He knew a lie when he heard it. Still, he couldn't get past the words. Or more to the point, the visual those words created.

He managed to keep his expression neutral, his voice steady. "It's okay, Jacqui. It was just a mix-up. Happens to the best of us."

Jacqui gave him a sassy smile, one that didn't quite reach her eyes. "Thanks for being so cool about it, Noah. You're a good guy."

Point to Jacqui. They were even. For now.

CHAPTER EIGHTEEN

"These are not your finest cuts, Mr. Mike. I don't know if I can pay top dollar for this."

"Your fault for running late today, Jacqui. Jed Winchester already got the best. But these are just as good."

Jacqui scowled at the name Jed Winchester but quickly fixed her face. One of the reasons she tried to get to the market at the crack of dawn was to thwart that man's efforts. If he thought he could roll into town with his untrained, backwoods cooking, he had another think coming.

Mike grinned down at her like he knew exactly what she was thinking and could see the dollar signs in her expression. He was a slightly overweight man with gray streaks highlighting his fiery red hair. There was a line of customers behind him. But he was in no hurry as he flashed a broad smile, his large forearms a testament to years of physical labor resting on the counter.

"Thirty percent off," Jacqui insisted.

Mike's reaction was immediate and theatrical. He clutched his heart as though struck by her words, his face a picture of mock horror. "Off? My meat? Next in line."

Jacqui didn't budge. No one tried to cut in front of her. This was their routine, a dance they performed each week, and he would have been disappointed by anything less.

The meat wasn't bad quality. It was still good. But Jacqui had to drive a hard bargain if she wanted to be respected in this industry. It had always been this way.

"Let's put aside that you sold your best cuts to an outsider."

"That outsider makes some good barbecue."

"And what's left here just doesn't look up to snuff. I think a little discount is in order."

"You're off your game this morning. Something to do with your wedding night?"

Jacqui did not blush. She would not blush. She glared.

"That would be my fault. Please excuse my wife."

My wife? It wasn't the first time Noah had said those words today. He'd used them when they'd stopped by the orchard stand and he chatted with Mr. Merchant about his Granny Smith apples. He'd used the title when they came up to the fishmonger, Mr. Phillips. The elderly man had been scaling today's catch, and Noah had asked about his knife. And now he'd used them again.

A shiver went down Jacqui's spine each time he said it. Why did those two words make her feel possessed by him? He wasn't even touching her.

Mike didn't miss anything. Not even as Jacqui ducked her head to examine the cuts for a third time. Noah put a hand on her waist. Jacqui jolted.

"Make it look real," Noah whispered in her ear. Then out loud, he said, "Are you going to introduce me to your friend, love?"

Love? That was even worse than *my wife.* That single word made her heart skip two beats.

"Mr. Mike, I think you should give my wife the newlywed discount," Noah was saying.

"I think I will. If she'll make her father's Dragon Ribs."

"I'll have that made up special for you if you throw in some pork belly." Jacqui held Mike's gaze. Neither of them flinched. She'd seen her father do this with Mike for years. She'd been practicing since she was thirteen. The practice paid off.

"This woman drives a hard bargain," Mike said, packing up the meat. "I'll put it on your tab."

Jacqui nodded as she reached for the package. Noah got there first. His long arms extended beyond hers, and Mike put the meat in his hands. Noah put the package into a reusable grocery bag. He'd been carrying all of her produce this morning.

"I thought you were wounded," Jacqui said when they were away from the butcher's stall. "From the bed last night."

A couple of coeds stopped and looked over their shoulders at the two of them. Jacqui lost the battle with her blush that time. Noah didn't bother to hide his smirk.

"I'm fine." Noah shrugged, not looking injured in the slightest. "These weigh nothing."

They meandered through the lively farmer's market. The air buzzed with the mingling scents of fresh herbs, ripe fruit, and the tantalizing aroma of freshly grilled food. People kept looking at them. Well, they were looking at him. Mostly women.

Women did outnumber men two to one in this town. Jacqui fought the urge to wrap her hands around his biceps.

Noah's steps slowed as they passed a popular food cart, its vibrant signage promising deep-fried delights. "Hey, let's grab something from here."

Jacqui wrinkled her nose, eyeing the food cart with a look of disdain. "A food cart? They're so unhygienic."

"You haven't eaten since breakfast."

She shrugged. She often didn't eat for stretches at a time. She had taken a tentative bite of the egg sandwich Noah had prepared and was surprised to find it tasty. Or maybe she'd just been that hungry. She'd barely eaten after the wedding and had gone to bed without eating at all.

She'd gone down to the kitchen to pop something into the microwave when she'd found him there. And then she'd found herself holding a spatula. Something that she'd done before learning to hold a pencil but hadn't done in years.

Jacqui snapped back to attention as Noah ordered a couple of the food cart's specialties. She heard her stomach grumble. The traitor. Jacqui watched closely as the cook prepared their food with an attention to detail that both surprised and impressed her. The sizzle of the meat as it hit the grill, the fresh aroma of baked bread, and the vibrant colors of locally sourced vegetables did more than just appeal to the senses—they told a story of passion and care similar to her own.

Jacqui loved everything about the food industry. She'd learned it all from her father and her grandfather. They'd wanted boys to carry on the restaurant's legacy. They'd gotten her. And even though the restaurant was more popular than ever, the bank account didn't reflect it. Mainly because the men in her family had tied up the money as they waited for Jacqui to marry.

When their orders were ready, they took their sandwiches to a nearby picnic table. Noah immediately dug into his order, making a satisfied sound that had Jacqui trying to gulp past that lump in her throat. She thought of the dream she had of tasting his lips. She thought of earlier in the morning when he'd offered.

"You wanna give it a try?" he asked.

"Beg your pardon?" she said.

Noah broke off a piece of his order and held it out to her. "Here. Try."

Normally, she would not have even dared. But it was like he was a genie granting her secret wish.

Jacqui wasn't sure if he moved closer or she leaned forward. She found herself next to him, her lips parting. And then the food was in her mouth.

Her taste buds instantly lit with the flavors of perfectly seasoned meat, tangy sauce, and crisp vegetables. She couldn't help the moan of appreciation that escaped her. She shot Noah a look of surprised approval.

"See? What did I tell you? Good, right?" Noah's voice was thick with satisfaction, his eyes crinkling with delight at her reaction.

She didn't answer. She didn't need to. He knew she liked it. She did, but why did she feel like she'd just lost a point in a game she didn't realize she was playing?

CHAPTER NINETEEN

*N*oah was going to win this game. Already he was racking up points. Not necessarily with his wife, but with her community. He'd schmoozed each and every vendor, farmer, butcher, and bystander they'd come across this morning. He knew her grandmother was already in his pocket—or maybe Noah was in her pocket. And her sister had looked at him like he was her hero when he'd rescued her fridge. The best friend hadn't cracked a smile yet, but he'd make her come around.

"Good, right?"

His attention was rapt on his wife's mouth as she bit down on his sandwich. A dollop of tangy barbecue sauce threatened to escape those kissable lips. Noah reached out with his thumb, catching it

SHANAE JOHNSON

just at the corner of her mouth. The contact was minimal but electrifying.

He felt Jacqui's sharp intake of breath. Her body tensed under the intimate touch. Her eyes widened, a flicker of something more than surprise—attraction, perhaps?—passing through them. Her nostrils flared, as if she was breathing in the moment, breathing in the sensation, breathing in him.

They were locked in a gaze that seemed to acknowledge the undercurrent of attraction that had been building between them. Then, almost as if embarrassed by the intimacy of the moment, Jacqui turned her head to chew and swallow her food, breaking the spell.

Noah watched her, a smile tugging at the corners of his lips. His heart pounded out a rhythm of hope. Yes, indeed, he was winning this game. He waited for her to meet his gaze again, the background noise of the market fading into a soft murmur around them.

Finally, Jacqui looked back at him, her cheeks slightly flushed, her expression one of defiance as if challenging the emotions that had just surfaced. Noah's smile widened as he took in his opponent. One day soon, she would realize they were on the same team.

"Are you going to return the favor? Can I have a bite of your food? It's only fair."

Jacqui's eyes narrowed, the corners of her mouth twitching upwards. She tore off a piece of her dish. Noah leaned forward, his lips parting. Jacqui pitched the food into his mouth, completely avoiding his lips.

He grinned as he bit down on the morsel, wishing it was her thumb. Or better yet, her bottom lip. Though her upper lip looked just as enticing.

As though to mock him, Jacqui sipped at her beverage. Noah glanced at it to see that it was a small carton of milk. A dollop of white cream coated her upper lip. Her tongue darted out, and she licked.

He coughed from the want of her. Then coughed again. Then again.

"What was in that?" He had to repeat himself. The first round of words were said hoarsely.

"Jalapeños."

"Crap."

"What? Too spicy for you?"

"Yeah," he said. Or at least he tried to say. He coughed again and then again. He took a deep breath, but only a few currents of air got past the wheeze.

A pat came on his back. "You okay?"

Noah couldn't speak. He'd never been good with spices. And Jacqui apparently liked it very, very hot. He pointed.

"What?" she asked, eyes getting large with concern.

He pointed again, jabbing his thumb at the carton that sat on the other side of her on the bench. Jacqui looked off toward the cart which was also on that side of her. Seeing he was getting nowhere—and desperately in need of relief—Noah reached for her milk.

He leaned over Jacqui's lap, catching a whiff of the cinnamon scent of her. His large hand wrapped around the small carton and brought it to himself. However, on the way to his mouth, he noticed the lightness of the small container. When he tipped it to his mouth, his worst fears were realized. It was empty.

Noah made another choking sound. He looked around desperately for relief. There was the food truck, but the *Back in Ten Minutes* sign was up. He could dash back into one of the booths at the farmer's market. Or there was a gas station in the distance. But right in front of him was Jacqui. And at the corner of her mouth was a dollop of cream.

It was a split second decision. It was a judgment

call to save his life. It wasn't like he had any other choices—any viable ones, anyway.

Noah wrapped his hand around his wife's neck and pulled her to him. At first, he went straight for the cream. It was sweet and took away some of the bite of the spicy dish.

He took another taste, this time including the entirety of the right corner of Jacqui's mouth. Her lips parted. Noah didn't hesitate. He was a trained soldier. He dove in head first.

His taste buds cooled, but the desire in him ran hot. He brushed his lips against hers, tasting the sweet flavor of cream that blended perfectly with the residual heat of her cinnamon taste. The spice of the moment between them bit back, hard and insistent.

Jacqui's hands found his shoulders, gripping them, pulling him closer, her own need and response mirroring his. The kiss deepened, driven by raw emotion and a connection that pulled them together. The world around them—the sounds of the farmer's market, the people, the colors—melted away until there was nothing but the two of them and the realization that what was happening was inevitable.

Noah had won, and he was lost. Lost in the sweet taste of his wife. Lost in the feel of her warm body against his. Lost in the hungry sounds that escaped her lips.

Jacqui's response lit up every nerve in his body. It was exactly what he had hoped for, yet a small voice in his mind reminded him of the strategy he'd considered earlier. If he wanted Jacqui to truly desire him, he needed to make her think the pursuit was hers. With regret lacing through him, Noah gently pulled away, his breaths shallow, his heart racing.

"Thanks for that," he said, his voice husky. "It cooled me right off."

CHAPTER TWENTY

"Tomatoes don't stack themselves, do they? And can someone tell me why the halibut is still not prepped?"

Jacqui's voice sliced through the busy clatter of the kitchen like a chef's knife through butter. She was standing in the center of her domain, the familiar clanking of pots and pans and the sharp tang of citrus doing little to soothe her frayed nerves. Her mind was still reeling from the kiss with Noah, a kiss that had scrambled every sensible thought inside her orderly brain into disarray.

As a chef, she prided herself on plating. Clean plating. None of that Jackson Pollock sauce splatter ever left her kitchen. But that's what it felt like inside her head since they'd left the farmer's market.

Noah trailed into the back door of the restaurant behind her. He carried the bags of produce in his arms. Setting them down by the prep station, his eyes scanned the bustling activity of the kitchen, then landed on Jacqui.

He didn't say anything. He didn't need to. He looked blankly at her. Because that kiss hadn't meant anything to him.

It had been a practical exercise. His mouth had been on fire. He'd needed milk to cool himself off. Completely logical.

Except it wasn't.

He'd done it on purpose. Hadn't he?

He'd done it to fluster her. Right?

He'd done it to get under her skin. Because he got some perverse joy from it. Well, Jacqui didn't have time for games. She had a job to do. And so did he.

"Mr. Henry, don't you—"

"Yes, Mrs. Henry?"

Jacqui blinked rapidly, like she couldn't quite focus on the man in front of her. The problem was, she saw him so clearly. Noah came into her personal space. He leaned over her like he was going to... he wasn't going to... he wouldn't dare to...

"Don't... don't you have some work to do?"

"I do, love." Noah inhaled deeply and slowly as he

leaned close to her. "Don't expect my best work. I gave you that last night."

There was a low whistle from behind them. The sizzle of meat staying too long on the fire. The crackle of something dropping into the heated oil.

Jacqui's mouth gaped. Noah took advantage of her shocked silence and pressed a quick kiss to her parted lips. Before she could react, before she could retaliate, before she could revel in the kiss, he disappeared in the back to his wires.

Jacqui took in a slow, shaky breath as she watched him go. She felt bested. It had been a long time since anyone got the better of her.

She balled her hands into fists to stop them from wanting. She pressed her lips together as though she could pulverize the sensations lingering from that kiss. Then she turned around.

Her crew jolted like cockroaches caught before a can of Raid.

"And why are these carrots looking like they've been chopped by a lawnmower? I need precision, people. We're creating fine dining cuisine here, not serving up a backyard barbecue."

The atmosphere in the kitchen shifted. The sizzle of the frying pans and the aromatic blend of spices in the air couldn't mask the sudden edge in Jacqui's commands. Her staff exchanged wary glances. Their movements became rigid under her sharp gaze.

"Uh, excuse me, Chef?"

Jacqui turned and came face to face with her young prep cook. Liam approached her with a cutting board laden with vegetables.

"Chef, could you check these julienne cuts for the garnish?"

The kid was still new to the kitchen, fresh out of a culinary program in high school with a framed certificate. He still had that novice smell about him; he didn't yet smell like fear.

Jacqui leaned over the cutting board, scrutinizing the thin strips of bell pepper that lay neatly aligned. "Too big," she said crisply, picking up one strip and holding it up for him to see. "For a garnish, we need delicacy. These are too robust."

She glanced around, spotting a clean knife. Her hand reached for it. But as her fingertips grazed the handle, her knuckles twitched. Her hand hovered over the handle, but as she gripped it, a slight tremor ran through her fingers. The knife felt alien, heavy, too real. With a barely perceptible sigh, she set it back down, masking her reaction with a quick, professional frown of a head chef who no longer needed to prep in their own kitchen.

"Hold the knife like this," Jacqui instructed, adjusting his grip. "You want to make confident, controlled cuts. Use your knuckles as a guide to keep the cuts consistent, and protect your fingers." She watched closely as Liam repositioned his hand according to her direction.

"Now try to slice through the pepper with a smooth, rolling motion," she continued, demonstrating the motion in the air with her own hand. "Apply just enough pressure to cut through the vegetable but keep it light enough to make thin, delicate strips. These are for garnishing, so they need to be fine and even."

Liam nodded, his eyes focused intently on the pepper as he tried again, this time with Jacqui's technique in mind. He carefully adjusted his stance and began slicing with a newfound precision. Jacqui observed, ready to give further guidance but pleased to see his immediate improvement.

"That's much better," Jacqui said approvingly after a few moments, examining the new batch of julienned peppers. "See how much more refined they look? That's what you're aiming for—a garnish that complements the dish, both visually and texturally."

"Yes, Chef."

Jacqui examined his work, her critical eye noting the precision in the cuts. "Good job, Liam."

Liam's face lit up with a proud grin at her praise. Jacqui couldn't bring herself to return the smile. She turned away, her heart heavy.

Cooking had once been her sanctuary, a place where she could lose herself in flavors and textures, where her hands confidently created and expressed her passion. But now each touch of the knife brought a surge of memories, a reminder of a time when the kitchen was her whole world. It wasn't just about the food; it was about who she had been when she was creating it.

She thought about the last dish she'd made in her parents' house. No child should be asked to make a parent's last meal. But she'd done it. And she hadn't picked up her knife since.

CHAPTER TWENTY-ONE

*N*oah wiped the sweat off his brow. The wiring work wasn't hard, it was just hot in here at the back of a full-service restaurant. Still, his movements were practiced and precise. The air around him buzzed not just with the hum of electricity, but with his own quiet anticipation.

The sun was starting to dip in the sky. He'd have to go home soon. Home with his wife. To her bed.

He had no doubt that he and Jacqui would start out on opposite sides of the mattress again. He had every faith that wouldn't last long. He'd seen her snuggle toward him and then into him in the middle of the night. Maybe tonight, he wouldn't keep his hands to himself.

Noah still tasted the sweet cream of milk from

her mouth. It soothed his tongue, his senses. A part of him couldn't wait to spark another flare of that spicy temper that he found so irresistibly charming.

He twisted the last of the copper wires together, securing them with a professional flick of his wrist. He was almost done with the job. He'd finish much sooner than anticipated.

Now his mind raced ahead, planning out the rest of his day, eager to see Jacqui. He mulled over what to say to her next. What comment might draw out that fire in her eyes that he was becoming so addicted to? Perhaps he'd tease her about her over-protective attitude toward the dessert menu, or maybe he'd rearrange the pens on her desk—anything to see the passion in her response. Or maybe he wouldn't say anything at all, and just sit quietly with her.

He could tell she needed that. Jacqui barked out so many orders, balanced the books, marshaled the livelihoods of all within these walls and some outside. She had a lot on her shoulders. Those slender shoulders and that swan's neck. He'd take off some of that load. Whether she liked it or not.

Lost in his thoughts and the rhythmic motion of his hands, Noah failed to notice that one of the wires had frayed. As he connected another wire to the junction box, his fingers brushed against the exposed copper. A sharp spark shot out, a bright burst of light accompanied by a biting snap.

Noah jerked his hand back in reflex, a sting of pain racing up his arm. He stared at his fingers, surprised by the sudden jolt. Then, almost involuntarily, a laugh bubbled up from his chest. He shook his head, amused at himself for getting caught off guard like that. Here he was, a seasoned handyman, daydreaming to the point of distraction— all because of a woman who'd turned his world delightfully upside down.

Shaking off the minor shock, Noah inspected his hand. It was fine, just a little singed, but it would serve as a funny story to share with Jacqui later. He could already imagine her scolding him for being careless, her brows furrowed in concern, masking the depth of her care for him, a care she was so reluctant to show.

He wrapped up the wiring, securing everything into place and ensuring no more exposed surprises. The small shock was a trivial price to pay for the joy that bubbled up in him now, living this new life. He anticipated returning to Jacqui's side— to tease, to provoke, to take care of her in a thousand small ways.

"What's going on with you two?"

"Ouch!" Noah banged his head against the fixture as he sat up too fast.

Fish stood in the doorway, a giant among men in the cramped space at the back of the kitchen. His old Army buddy had been an immovable force back in the service. He still was now. His broad shoulders were comically wide as they filled the entire frame of the door. The top of his head, adorned with a mop of thick, dark hair, brushed against the frame. His imposing figure was more suited to a battlefield than the tight workings within a kitchen. Yet there he was, an essential part of the restaurant's crew.

"I told you what's going on," Noah said, keeping his voice low. He didn't play dumb and ask who Fish was talking about. The only person he was hiding his true feelings from was his wife. "It was love at first sight. You were there."

Fish regarded his friend with the eyes of an interrogator. They'd gone through the same SERE training together. Noah knew that survival and evasion might be difficult when faced with someone equally adept at resistance and escape. Especially when that someone held a sharp paring knife in his large paw.

"There's something going on between you two." A

pinging sound sliced through the air as Fish ran the blade over a sharpening stone.

"You think I'd kiss and tell about my wife?"

"Your wife." It wasn't a question. It was a statement. A definitive one.

"Yeah. My wife."

Packing up his tools, Noah felt Fish's gaze on him. The look was pointed and unmistakably suspicious. It was a gaze that Noah knew well, one that they had shared often in the field when something didn't add up. Fish's eyes, sharp and assessing, bored into him, trying to decipher what Noah was up to with all the hurry in his actions.

In the Army, Fish's size had always been an advantage, a visual deterrent as much as a physical one. Here, in the civilian life of a small town, it made him stand out, but not uncomfortably so.

"Just be careful with these Chou women. They're all fiercely independent. The kind that are prone to keep boys on the side."

Now Noah knew what this was about. He'd seen how Fish looked at Jules. "That's the thing, my friend. Neither one of us are boys. And neither one of us is small enough to fit on the side."

Noah met Fish's scrutinizing look. There was a comfort in being understood so well by someone who had been through the same trials and tribulations, someone who knew all the facets of his character.

"Now if you'll excuse me, I have to go find my wife and get her home for dinner. You, on the other hand, look like you need some sugar-free dessert."

CHAPTER TWENTY-TWO

*J*acqui let out a long breath as she stepped out from the bustling kitchen into the main dining area, where the lively chatter of patrons mixed with the clinks of cutlery and the savory aromas of Chinese fusion dishes. Her demeanor transformed as soon as she crossed the threshold; the stern, demanding chef became a gracious hostess, her smile wide and genuine as she approached the first table of regulars.

"Evening, Bill, Anne," Jacqui greeted warmly, her eyes sparkling with recognition. "How are we enjoying the new pork belly bao buns tonight?"

Bill, a robust man with a hearty laugh, wiped his mouth with a napkin before answering. "Jacqui, these are out of this world. I swear, the way you fuse those flavors, it's like a dance on the taste buds."

Jacqui didn't correct him that she wasn't the one fusing the flavor. It had been her idea. But not her handiwork. The garnish Liam had chopped had gone into the dish, though, and was now being scarfed down by the ravenous diner.

Anne, ever the culinary enthusiast, chimed in, her voice animated. "And the slaw. It's got just the right kick. How do you balance it so perfectly?"

Even though she hadn't chopped, stir-fried, or sautéed any part of the meal, it still was her dish. She took pride in the hard work and critical eye that got it to the table. "It's all about finding the harmony, just like in a good song. A little bit of Yankee twang with a dash of Sichuan spice, and voilà." She gestured with a flourish, her hands expressive.

"We heard about your marriage. Is it true?"

"It... I... I have to welcome some new customers." Jacqui moved on to a table with new customers, her smile just as welcoming. "Welcome to Chow Town. I'm Jacqui, the chef. Is this your first time dining with us?"

The couple, clearly taken by the unique ambiance, nodded enthusiastically. "Yes, and everything looks so inviting," the woman said, her gaze sweeping over the menu.

"If you're looking for something truly unique, I'd recommend our blackened catfish with ginger-infused collard greens," Jacqui suggested, her voice laced with a hint of a challenge, as if daring them to dive into the culinary adventure she had crafted after one of her calls with Jami.

When Jami had called her from Beijing last year, she'd called to gush about the catfish dish with Jacqui while she was still inside the restaurant. Jami was excellent at describing dishes to such detail that the other person could imagine each spice. Only in Jacqui's imagination, the dish needed something American added to it. That's when the greens came in.

As she conversed with the young couple, Jacqui kept a watchful eye on the rest of the dining room, her senses sharply attuned to the needs of her guests. Many eyes were on her. She saw people talking from behind their menus, likely about her new marriage. She avoided those tables of people she knew, especially people she knew who gossiped behind their tea cups.

When Jacqui noticed a slight frown on a patron's

face, she excused herself from the newcomers with a promise of returning shortly. Approaching the concerned diner, Jacqui softened her expression to one of concern. "Everything all right with your meal?"

"Oh, yes, it's delicious." The man wore a pressed collar shirt that had seen better days. His jeans had a bit of a smudge on the knees. He was clearly a working class guy. He leaned in as he continued talking to Jacqui, his voice lowered as though he didn't want to offend. "But could we possibly get a little extra hoisin sauce?"

"Absolutely, I'll have it right out for you," Jacqui assured him.

She picked up the bottle from another table and brought it back to him. She didn't get in the least bit offended when the diner splayed the sauce all over his dish. Her grandfather would've been appalled that his carefully crafted food had been altered. Food was the one area where Jacqui let go of the reins. If they wanted to add more salt, so be it. If they decided to put ketchup on their lo mein... Well, there she drew the line.

Leaving behind the satisfied customer, Jacqui turned and headed toward the kitchen. But she barely got a few steps in when she ran into a wall. A warm wall that smelled of cut wood and spring grass. She didn't have to look up to know who was there.

Her nose remembered curling into his scent. Her palms remembered resting over his heartbeat. Her head found that spot in his chest where it fit perfectly, like it was made for her.

"There are the newlyweds," said Anne.

Instead of walking backward to release her, Noah wrapped an arm around Jacqui's waist, like it was his business to do so. Like it was his right to do so. Jacqui couldn't sneak away from him or shake him off because everyone was watching. So she plastered a smile on her face.

"Are you going to introduce me to everyone, love?" Noah said the words against her ear but loud enough for everyone to hear.

Jacqui had to take a minute to let the shiver from the heat of his breath at the cone of her ear run down her neck, across her shoulder blades and down to the base of her spine before she found her voice. "I don't want to interrupt everyone's meals."

There was a chorus of *nonsense* and *no*'s and *pleases*. Just like the nosy neighbors they were.

Noah looked down at her with such adoration in his eyes that it made her breath catch. She looked up into his eyes, seeing warmth and affection reflected back at her. But it wasn't genuine. It couldn't be.

Gathering herself under the watchful eyes of her patrons, Jacqui managed a smile. "Everyone, this is Noah, my husband."

Noah's fingers flexed when she said those two words: *my husband.* He pulled her a little closer. His breath hitched as he pressed a kiss to her temple.

There went his hot breath again. And there went that shiver again. But instead of going down, this time it went straight to her head.

Jacqui swallowed and began again. "He's been working tirelessly on updating our old wiring and making sure we don't burn down from an electrical fire," she joked lightly, eliciting chuckles from the surrounding tables.

"That's how we met," said Noah. "Sparks flew. I apologize if there were any power outages that night."

There was a chorus of *ahhs.* He was good. A little too good.

"It's great to meet all of you. But I need to get my wife home. We are newlyweds, after all."

"Oh honey." Jacqui's fake grin was tense. "There's still work to do."

"Yes, but that work needs to be done in private."

He nuzzled at her neck, which effectively shut her up.

It did not shut everyone else up. Now there was a chorus of juvenile *ohhhs*. In the distraction of it all, Noah managed to tug Jacqui out the front door.

CHAPTER TWENTY-THREE

*N*oah's hand lingered at the small of Jacqui's back as they moved toward the exit of Chow Town. Her delicate scent filled his senses each time he leaned in to nuzzle her neck. And he did it at every opportunity, which he knew she only allowed because her patrons *oohed* and *ahhed* as the two newlyweds strolled by.

Each soft touch of his lips to her nape was a whispered promise. Each strum of his fingers at her lower back was a gesture of possession he needed Jacqui to understand and a claiming he needed the men of this town to heed. The diners they passed watched with soft smiles and quiet sighs, their eyes twinkling with the joy of witnessing what they believed was a tender moment between a loving couple.

The warmth of Jacqui's body so close to his, the subtle cinnamon fragrance of her hair, and the way she occasionally leaned back into him—all of it made Noah's heart thrum with a hopeful rhythm. Instead of pushing away from him, Jacqui met his caresses with a slight, almost imperceptible relaxation in her shoulders, suggesting a comfort with his closeness that went beyond their public charade.

Behind them, the sounds of the restaurant faded into a soft backdrop of clinking glasses and subdued conversations, punctuated by the occasional sigh from a patron enchanted by the scene they presented. Noah knew this moment was just for show, a display for the eyes of their small-town community, yet every second that Jacqui didn't pull away felt like a victory, a step closer to something real.

When they reached the exit, Noah prepared himself for the shift he knew was coming—the moment they stepped out of sight of the diners, when the warmth would drop away and the space between them would grow cold again. He braced himself, his gut twisting in anticipation of the loss.

All while planning for his next move when they got home.

But as Jacqui pushed open the exit door, a soft sigh escaped her lips, so faint he might have imagined it. It wasn't a sigh of relief or a release of pent-up performance. It was different—tinged with a note of something like regret or longing. Noah allowed himself to wonder, to hope.

Could it be that Jacqui felt the stirrings of something genuine? That beneath the reminders of their arrangement and the boundaries she so firmly set, there might be a desire for something real?

They stepped out into the cool evening air, the quiet of the outside world enveloping them after the buzz of the restaurant. That's when he felt it; the tension returned to Jacqui's posture. Her body stiffened as she prepared to distance herself once more. Yet that single, soft sigh hung between them like a question left unanswered.

Jacqui turned to face him, her expression unreadable in the dim light. "You can stop the show. We're out of everyone's sight."

"Maybe I was enjoying the show, too."

Her eyes flashed in the evening light. "Too?"

Noah knew he should pull back. This wasn't the

plan. But this wasn't the first time he'd come in hot on a live wire.

"Maybe I like the way you taste," he said. "Maybe I want another bite."

Jacqui's throat worked. Her gaze dropped to his mouth. That swan's neck of hers tilted back, like she could already feel his lips against her skin.

Noah took a step forward, ready to lay claim to the prize that was his wife.

"And here I thought she married you for her money."

That brought him up short. They both turned to see Nãinai walking toward them, leaning heavily on a bejeweled cane. Noah wasn't so sure the old woman needed that cane. He'd bet it was for show.

"Isn't it past your bedtime, Nãinai?" said Jacqui.

"Don't be sassy when I come bearing gifts." The older woman held up a folio of documents. "This will release your inheritance to you."

The night was warm, but at that moment a chill breeze whispered through the parking lot. An owl hooted a somber call. The scent of spice wafted toward them from the restaurant as the doors opened and closed. The heat of the spice almost had Noah choking.

He watched as Jacquie's fingers flexed, eager to grab at her financial freedom. He'd thought this wasn't coming for months. But here it was.

"There's also the document for one share of the restaurant in there," said Nãinai, her gaze moving from Jacqui's wide-eyed wonder to Noah's narrowed glare.

Noah got the sense that just like this woman didn't need the cane to support her, she knew she was shaking things up between him and Jacqui. But why? What was her end game?

"That gives you girls forty-nine percent interest in the restaurant," said Jacqui, her fingers curling around the paperwork and then bringing it into her chest.

Again Noah scowled. Those papers were resting where he wanted to be. He wanted to be the one curled into her chest. He wanted to be the one who came to her rescue.

"When both of your sisters marries, then you girls will have the controlling interest," Nãinai was saying.

What Noah knew was that he didn't have control in this situation anymore. He thought he'd have more time. Now that Jacqui had everything she wanted and he was finished with the wiring job, she didn't need him anymore.

He just couldn't let her know that. He wasn't ready to be done with her. He knew he never would be.

CHAPTER TWENTY-FOUR

*J*acqui sat in the passenger seat of Noah's truck. Her fingers unconsciously played with the edge of the envelope she held. Inside was a significant infusion of funds for Chow Town and more control over the culinary empire she was determined to build.

She could make updates. She could redesign the dining area. She could even afford to shut down for a week to do it. This should have been one of the happiest days of her professional life, yet there was a hollow feeling inside her that she couldn't quite shake.

She stole a glance at Noah. He was focused on the road, his jaw set in a way that told her he was carrying his own set of worries. The lines around his eyes seemed deeper today, like they were etched by a mixture of fatigue and something else—perhaps reluctance? She couldn't help but wonder if, now that the restaurant was finally on stable financial footing, he would feel his job here was done. The thought that he might leave, that he could very well step out of her life as seamlessly as he had stepped in, pressed down on her chest like a physical weight.

But that's what she wanted, right?

That was the deal, right?

They pulled up in front of her house. The engine's gentle rumble cut off as Noah shifted into park. The silence that settled between them was heavy, filled with unspoken questions and silent answers.

He turned to her, his expression softening as he caught her eye. Then it hardened. "Wait until I get your door."

Jacqui nodded, biting the corner of her lip. His gaze dipped down to track the movement. She let go of her lip, and a sigh escaped.

Noah tore his gaze away from her mouth. She thought she might have heard a muttered curse as he punched open his door and climbed out.

She watched him walk around the truck, his movements deliberate, always so mindful of her in these small, considerate ways. When he opened her door, the evening air brushed against her skin, carrying with it the subtle scent of blooming jasmine from her garden, a reminder of home and something resembling peace.

"Thanks," she said as she stepped out, her voice softer than she intended. Her feet touched the ground, but it was his steady presence that grounded her more than the concrete beneath her shoes.

Noah closed the door behind her and lingered, looking like he was debating whether to say more. They walked silently to the door. He stayed a step behind her, a quiet shadow that was part protector with a touch of what felt like a stalker.

But that couldn't be right. He was just here to do a job. Just here for the money. And then he'd go.

They marched up the porch steps in tandem. Coming face to face with the locked front door, Jacqui didn't wait for him to hold out his hand for her keys. She just held them up between them. Noah took the proffered key ring from her. Rough calluses brushed over the back of her finger, lingering at her polished nail before releasing her.

"I suppose I should get you your own set," she hedged.

The key scraped against the lock as he tensed. Oh

no, had she said the wrong thing? He was probably already mentally packing.

"You want me to stay?" he asked.

"You need to finish the wiring." But he'd mentioned he was almost done. "And the additional work at my sister's place."

He nodded, stepping aside so she could enter through the open door. But not before he did a sweep of the entryway and turned on the lights. It had to be his military training, but she liked it.

The sound of the door locking behind her was loud. Jacqui liked the notion of being trapped inside with him. It made all worries lift from her head and fly away. But really, what worries did she have left?

She had the money from her trust fund. The wiring was nearly done. Her sisters were in good health and now would want for nothing with the cash infusion in the envelope in her hands.

Noah took her bag from her and hung it on the rack. With the weight of her satchel gone, she felt even lighter.

"Did you eat?" he asked.

Jacqui pursed her lips, trying to remember what she consumed aside from tasting a few sauces before approving them to be served.

Noah sighed, but he didn't sound put out. "I'll heat up something."

"You don't have to."

"What kind of husband would I look like if my chef-wife starved?"

"Just be wary of the ketchup. Don't want anything too spicy for you."

"Ha, ha." Noah grinned.

Jacqui grinned.

He was walking backward toward the kitchen, not taking his eyes off her. That's when he paused.

"What's that?" he asked.

Jacqui winced. "I had it delivered while we were out."

He glared at the king-sized package outside the guest bedroom. But he didn't say anything.

"I figured you'd, you know, want it."

His gaze snapped back to her. He looked at her almost like he wanted her instead of the new bed she'd had delivered.

"I'm not tired," he said.

"Me neither," she said hurriedly. "I was going to watch some TV for a while. On the couch."

"Mind if I join you?"

"Sure. Okay."

CHAPTER TWENTY-FIVE

*N*oah stood in Jacqui's kitchen, perplexed as he rummaged through her freezer. He was baffled to find an array of frozen foods —frozen pizzas, frozen waffles, frozen rice, frozen vegetables. It made no sense.

No chef he'd ever encountered would counte- nance foods seasoned with frost bite. Aside from that, he'd been with Jacqui this morning at the farmer's market. All of those bags of produce had been taken to the restaurant. None had been brought to her home.

"Why do you have all these frozen meals when you're such a stickler for freshness at Chow Town?"

Jacqui leaned against the kitchen counter, popping the corner of a pizza crust in her mouth.

"This is the only time I get to enjoy my favorite childhood foods without anyone judging my culinary choices."

She didn't meet his gaze as she chewed. A touch of red heated her cheeks as she swallowed. She allowed the curtain of her hair to fall into her face, effectively shielding her from him.

Noah would let her hide. This time. He fully intended to find out what dimmed the light inside his wife's eyes when it came to cooking.

"You do realize these are packed with sodium and all sorts of processed ingredients, right?" He nudged the bag of tater tots. "I'm sure it's against chef law to harbor such a fugitive."

"You can't tell anyone." Jacqui's gaze lifted. Her voice rang with mock seriousness. "Spouses can't testify against one another in a court of law."

His grin was bright enough to light up the kitchen. It was reflected back at him in a flash of her teeth. Those gleaming teeth tugged at the corner of her lip. Noah swore to the culinary gods that he was going to bite that lip before the night was done.

"You should have tried the MREs we had in the military. I'm pretty sure those things are designed to survive a nuclear apocalypse."

Now it was Jacqui's eyes that widened in mock

horror. "Well, if you survived MREs, I think you can handle my frozen pizza and tater tots tonight."

She was playing with him. He would walk across a mine-covered playground if it meant he would be met with this side of Jacqui. He couldn't take his eyes off this more relaxed, playful side of his wife. She was barefoot, her hair down in soft waves that framed her face, making her look more approachable and, if possible, even more beautiful.

"I suppose tomorrow it's back to quinoa salads and perfectly balanced vinaigrettes?" Noah spread out the bounty ice box treats on the countertop.

"Don't forget the tofu."

Noah moaned at the threat of the plant-based protein. He'd had it for lunch earlier this week. But only because he hadn't known what he was eating. After the first bite, he'd known it wasn't meat. However, it had been tasty. When Jacqui had happened upon him and told him what he was putting into his mouth, he had the thought of spitting it out. He hadn't because it was really, really good. Though he hadn't dared admit that.

Jacqui approached the counter where Noah had laid out the pizza, her hands slightly trembling as she reached for the pizza cutter. Noah noticed the subtle shake. It wasn't the first time he'd seen her fingers tremble when face to fingertips with a kitchen utensil.

It had happened earlier this morning when he'd made breakfast and she'd picked up the spatula. Come to think of it, he had never seen her in the Chow Town kitchen preparing any food. He moved closer, placing his hands gently over hers to steady them.

Looking up into his eyes, Jacqui bit at the corner of her lips again. Then her lips parted. Her tongue darted out to moisten her upper lip, as though she was preparing to send words across.

Noah got the sense these would be important words, like she was on the verge of sharing something profound. Her gaze flickered with a vulnerability Noah hadn't seen. He sensed there was something significant she was wrestling with.

Before Jacqui could voice her thoughts, the oven timer dinged sharply, signaling that the tater tots were ready. The moment broke, and with it, the chance for her to reveal her burdens.

Jacqui managed a laugh, slipping back into the more familiar role of the unflappable chef. "I told you I wouldn't cook for you, but I also won't serve you. You can grab those while I get the plates."

She turned on her heel. Noah caught the exhale

she released when her back was turned. He spied the clench and release of her fingers before she went up on tiptoes to reach for the plates.

Jacqui inhaled again. This time it was at the contact of Noah's fingertips on her low back.

"Let me," he said, reaching for the cabinet and bringing down the plates. "We're home now. You should relax."

"Okay." Her voice was shaky on just those two syllables. And there was that tremble again. Right there in her right hand. She clenched and unclenched her fists. Then she put her hands behind her back and looked up at Noah. "Have you decided what you want to watch?"

"I'm happy to watch whatever you like."

She gave a curt nod, then went to pick up the platter of food.

"No, no. I got it."

"You keep leaving me with nothing to do," she said. There was confusion in her gaze, as though she didn't know what to do when responsibilities got taken from her.

"Go have a seat. Get comfortable."

Jacqui did as she was told. When Noah came into the living room, she sat in the corner of the couch. Her feet were tucked beneath her. Noah could've chosen the opposite corner. But he wasn't going to pass up the opportunity to be close to his wife. He took the middle cushion.

"What are we watching?" he asked as he arranged food on a small plate for her. "Not the Cooking Channel, since you're off work and you need to let your brain unwind."

He blew on the hot slice of pizza. Then he lifted it to her mouth.

At first she startled at the offering. Then she glared suspiciously at him. Noah waited patiently, not moving a muscle until she accepted what he gave her.

Jacqui leaned forward and took a bite. Noah watched her lips move as she chewed.

"I don't care to watch anything military, either." He dipped a tater tot in ketchup, then held it out to her.

There was no glare this time. There was a pause. It lasted half a second, less than the last time. Then she leaned in and took his offering.

Noah scooted closer. "How about a reality show so we can make fun of people making the wrong decisions about their lives?"

Jacqui's throat worked as she swallowed the pizza and tot. Then she nodded. She rested back against the cushions but not in the corner. She rested closer to him, meeting in the middle.

Noah continued to feed her, bit by bit. It never occurred to him that he hadn't taken a single bite of food the whole time. His belly didn't grumble from hunger. He slowed its beats in complete contentment as Jacqui moved closer and closer into his heat.

CHAPTER TWENTY-SIX

*S*he knew she wasn't dreaming. And it was all the more perfect that this was really happening to her. Because this was something she had never even thought to want for herself.

In the soft predawn light that barely hinted at the new day outside, Jacqui lay perfectly still, wrapped in the warmth of Noah's arms. She considered allowing herself to believe she was still caught in the tendrils of a dream, because if she was in a dream, then she would give herself permission to do the things there that she would never do in reality. The reality, however, was just so much better than she could imagine.

There was the solid feel of Noah's chest against

her back. His breathing was rhythmic and soothing as it brushed against her neck. One of his hands rested at the divot of her hip. The other was draped around her neck, his thumb on her pulse point. This was nothing the fabrication of her sleep-addled mind could produce; this was wonderfully, terrifyingly real.

As consciousness nudged her further awake, Jacqui savored the memory of the previous evening —the way Noah had taken care of her, effortlessly stepping into the role of host in her own home. He had fed her slices of the frozen pizza and tater tots. They'd clicked through episodes of a reality show and mocked the participants mercilessly. Jacqui wasn't sure when it had happened, but he had ultimately drawn her into the curve of his body. Or maybe she had snuck past his defenses to find a hiding spot there.

The way he smelled, a mix of clean linen and something distinctly Noah, was now a scent she would recognize anywhere, a scent that spoke of safety and something perilously close to home. The temperature of his skin was just right, warmer than any blanket. His heat seeped into her in a way that loosened the knots of tension that perpetually wound through her shoulders and back.

Lying there on her couch, Jacqui felt a peace she hadn't known in years. It was nothing like her usual mornings, which were filled with immediate thoughts of to-do lists and the day's responsibilities. Here, in the quiet of her living room with Noah, she found a tranquility that whispered seductive promises of what could be if she let her guard down completely.

But as the first true light of morning began to seep through the curtains, reality beckoned with the subtlety of a sledgehammer. She knew she had to open her eyes, had to slip from the sanctuary of Noah's arms and face the world that awaited her.

When she opened her eyes, it was to a message on the television screen. Netflix asked if she still wanted to watch. On the table sat the last remnants of their frozen meal: the crusts of frozen pizza and a few tots covered in ketchup. At the edge of the table sat the envelope that Nāinai had handed to Jacqui.

That envelope made it possible for Jacqui to have everything she'd ever dreamed of. The restaurant could get its upgrades. Jules' bakery could expand. Jami could stay on the road longer. But what did it get Jacqui? What did she want?

What she wanted was to stay exactly where she was. She wanted to keep Noah's arms around her.

She wanted him to heat her up some breakfast and then feed it to her while she sat in his lap. That was too much to ask for.

Reluctantly, Jacqui pushed off him. She did not get far.

Noah's hold tightened. His eyes were already open, heavy with sleep, but quick to focus on her. His voice was rough with sleep but filled with a warmth that echoed in his eyes. "Morning."

"Morning." Her voice was barely above a whisper. The space between them was charged with an unspoken acknowledgment of the night's intimacy and the day's demands.

His hair was tousled, his expression one of content understanding, as if he too wished they could linger in the night's shadow. Jacqui offered Noah a smile that carried a silent thank you for the night, for the care, for the momentary escape. Surely, he'd be ready to move on soon. He had a life he'd want to get back to.

As she prepared to rise from the couch, he captured her hand. It was the one where he'd placed a ring. His thumb pressed against that band.

"Why don't you take the day off?" he said.

"I can't do that."

"You think your boss wouldn't allow it?"

"I'm my boss."

He raised his brows.

She bit her lip.

He tracked the movement. "Spend the day with me."

"You have work to do, too."

"I finished the wiring job last night."

Something sank in her belly. He was done. He had no reason to stay.

"I saw some other repairs I want to make after I finish with your sister's bakery. But they're not urgent."

"How much are you going to charge me for those?"

"One day off," he said each word deliberately like it was its own sentence. "With your husband. The more you hesitate, the more interest I'm going to charge you."

"Interest?"

He nodded solemnly. "One kiss for every hesitation."

Her lips parted.

Noah moved closer. He moved slowly, giving her the opportunity to back away. Or to say no. Jacqui did neither.

The corner of his mouth lifted higher with each

inch as he came closer. His approach was deliberate and unhurried, giving her every chance to back away or to voice any objections. The familiar scent of him —clean soap mixed with a hint of citrus from his cologne—filled her senses. Jacqui found herself rooted to the spot, anticipation tingling across her skin.

"Why do you want to kiss me, Noah?"

"Because I didn't get to dessert last night."

When Noah was just a breath away, he paused, his eyes searching hers for any sign of reluctance. Jacqui consciously held herself still. She kept her features as they were, not wanting to show him any sign that she didn't want what was about to happen.

Noah got the hint. But he didn't pounce. He continued his slow assault.

He leaned in, his breath mingling with hers, a prelude to the promised kiss. Jacqui closed her eyes, the world narrowing down to the sensation of his breath on her face, warm and slightly uneven, as if he were just as affected by this moment as she was.

Then his lips met hers. Soft and tentative at first, as if he was savoring the moment before deepening the kiss. The sensation was electric, sparking a warmth that radiated through her entire body. His lips were gentle yet insistent, moving against hers in a rhythm that felt achingly familiar. The taste of him was just as intoxicating. So much so that it drew a soft moan from her throat.

Noah's hands found her waist, pulling her closer until there was no space left between them, his touch firm yet tender. She could just make out the faint sounds of the world around them—the distant chirping of birds, the soft rustle of leaves in the breeze. It was all drowned out by the rushing of blood in her ears and the thudding of her heart.

The kiss deepened, and Jacqui's senses were overwhelmed by him. The feel of his strong hands steadying her. The sight of his eyelashes fluttering closed just before their lips met again, and then again. The sound of a soft sigh that escaped him as he pressed her more tightly against his chest.

Reluctantly breaking the kiss, Jacqui opened her eyes to find Noah watching her. There was a satisfied look on his face. Yet there was also a question in his eyes.

"You got your dessert," she said.

"What if I want more?"

Breathless and a little dazed, Jacqui reached up to touch her lips, still tingling from his kiss. In answer to his question, she nodded her head. This time it was Jacqui who dipped her head to meet his mouth. But before she could take hold of his lips, the door-bell rang.

CHAPTER TWENTY-SEVEN

*N*oah tapped out a rhythmic beat on the steering wheel. Better that he take out his frustration on his car than reach over and claim his wife like he truly wanted to do. Though he was now convinced that she just might possibly not rebuff his advances. Maybe?

Beside him in the passenger seat, Jacqui sat glancing out the window. Her hair was loose and down around her shoulders. She wore a sundress that hugged those curves that had lain snuggled up against Noah in the midnight hours on the couch last night. Her fingers absently tugged at her lower lip—an unconscious gesture that spoke volumes about her lingering thoughts on their unfinished kiss just an hour ago.

The moment had been electric, their connection a live wire that had intensified with each passing second until the abrupt ring of the doorbell had shattered it. An Amazon driver with a package had never been so untimely or unwelcome. The interruption had cast a subtle chill over the warmth they'd been basking in, shifting the mood from intimate to interrupted.

Noah knew the potential of what could have been a lingering, deepening kiss. The thought of reclaiming that lost moment fueled a determined optimism in him. He turned his gaze back to the road, planning, scheming ways to recreate the magic that morning had promised.

He'd only had a taste of the dessert tray that was Jacqui Chou Henry. He was done sampling. Noah had every plan to sit down at the table for the main course herself.

The light morning traffic hummed around them, a mundane backdrop to the charged silence that filled the car. As the traffic light turned green, he stole another glance at Jacqui. The soft morning light caught her profile, highlighting her contemplative expression. He wanted to reach out, to bridge the gap with words or touch, but he also recognized the value of patience, of giving her space to process the morning's swift shift from intimate to ordinary.

"Busy day ahead?" he ventured, breaking the silence.

Jacqui turned from the window, her eyes meeting his briefly before focusing on the road ahead. The blush that spread across her cheeks was even better than the sparks when they argued. "Yeah, I have a few things to sort out at the restaurant."

"I thought we were taking the day off."

She let out a weary sigh. "I can't just take time off."

"You have a head chef, prep cooks, and a saucer."

A grin split her lips. "Saucier."

"Not sure a man like Aarav would appreciate being called sassy. But that's my opinion."

This time, a giggle escaped the grin. Jacqui pinched her lower lip again. Then she tugged it into her mouth, never losing hold of the smile Noah had coaxed from her.

"My point is, the restaurant will be fine. Besides, if you really want to work, we can check out the competition."

She opened her mouth and closed it. Then she looked out the window to see that they were driving past Chow Town. "Hey! This is kidnapping."

"A husband can't kidnap his wife." That wasn't precisely true. But Noah doubted anyone would argue with him. By the time the day was over, and if he played his cards right, it wouldn't be charges his wife would want to press against him.

Jacqui pursed her lips. When she opened her mouth, it was clear to see that Noah had won. "I have to stop at the bank first."

She looked down at the envelope in her lap. In there was her key to freedom—financially speaking. Jacqui worried the edges of the envelope, then used the same fingers to worry at her lip. She could've told him that his services were no longer needed. She didn't. Because she wanted more of his kisses. She likely didn't know how to ask. This one time, he would take it easier on her.

He pulled up into the bank's parking lot. Bringing the vehicle to a stop, he put it in park and turned to face his wife. At the same time, she turned to face him.

"Jacqui—"

"Noah—"

"You go first," they both said at the same time.

"Ladies first."

"That's a ridiculous notion. Just because I'm a woman, I go first."

"Because you're my wife, you go first."

That wiped the smile off her face. "But I'm not really. Your wife, I mean."

"I've got a legal document that says differently. It entitles me to put you ahead of me."

"It also entitles you to half of what's mine." Jacqui's hands tightened on the envelope.

"You still think I'm in this for the money?"

"I..." She hesitated, hand flexing and releasing the envelope. Only to tighten around it again.

Noah let go of the steering wheel. Just in time, his right hand clamped around his left wrist, holding himself back from grabbing his wife to him like some kind of Neanderthal—though he felt more like a Cro-Magnon at the moment.

"You realize I charged half the normal rate and did double the work in a quarter of the time? Why do you think I did that, Jacqui?"

Jacqui's gaze was fixated on his left hand, like she knew what that hand wanted to do to her. Like she wasn't so sure she wouldn't like it. "Because of Fish. Some kind of Army code or something."

"Hmmm." Noah massaged his wrist, but he didn't let go. Not yet. "Just like I hovered around Fish's office to catch a glimpse of him. Or found any reason—even a fight—just so I could speak with him. Or made sure that he ate and took a break after a long day on his feet. Yeah, I did all that for the Army code thing I share with Fish."

"I don't know what you're doing with me." Jacqui threw up her hands, the envelope falling to the floor. "Everyone always wants something from me. I can't figure out what you want. You don't ask me for anything. And you drive me crazy."

Noah leaned over, placing one hand on either side of the headrest until he crowded her in the passenger seat. "Maybe that's what I want: to drive you so crazy that you break the guest room bed so that you have to sleep next to me. To watch bad television with you until you curl up in my arms where you belong."

Both their breaths came as though they'd run a marathon. Because they both had. It had only been a week, but Noah felt like he'd been racing his whole life to get to this point. To get to this woman.

"What I want from you, Jacqui, is just you. I want you."

There was confusion in her gaze. But also desire. It was enough for Noah. He inched closer. But not close enough to take. He needed her to take that last step.

"Let me have you."

"What are you going to do with me?" Her lips brushed his as she spoke, but she didn't press into him. She was still holding back.

"I'm going to take care of you."

And with that, he pulled away and got out of the vehicle. By the time he rounded to her side and handed her out, it was clear she was off balance. Perfect, just the way he wanted her. As she walked into the bank with unsteady feet, Noah kept his hand at her low back, providing the support she could no longer deny she needed.

CHAPTER TWENTY-EIGHT

*J*acqui's mind was adrift, still echoing with the soft pressure of Noah's lips against hers, the sensation lingering like a sweet note in a favorite song. He hadn't kissed her. Not exactly. He'd just whispered the promise of it. Jacqui had wanted to make that promise into a vow. But she'd realized it too late, and he'd been gone.

Only he wasn't gone. He was right beside her. He held her hand in his as they walked down the familiar paths of her hometown, his fingers intertwined tightly with hers. Jacqui felt anchored in a way that she never had before. Not since her parents had held her hand, given her a hug, planted a kiss on her forehead.

Noah was the anchor in the current that was her whirling thoughts. She followed him, letting him guide her through the town with a calm assurance. Jacqui pointed out the old bookstore where she'd spent countless hours as a child, the bench by the river where she used to read and dream. Each site was a memory, a piece of her past. Yet as she shared these slivers of her life, she found herself oddly tongue-tied. Words, usually her friends, now stumbled and tripped on her tongue.

They passed Mrs. Dalloway's flower shop. Jacqui waved to the elderly owner, who was arranging a colorful display of spring blooms outside.

"Jacqui, dear, who is this handsome young man?" Mrs. Dalloway called out.

Noah stepped forward with a charming smile, his grip on Jacqui's hand tightening reassuringly. "I'm Noah, Jacqui's husband," he introduced himself smoothly, taking the lead as he always did.

"Ah, lucky man." Mrs. Dalloway clapped her hands delightedly. "You keep her happy, you hear?"

"I intend to," Noah replied, his gaze drifting back to Jacqui with a look so filled with warmth it made her heart flutter uncontrollably.

They continued their stroll with Noah pausing to admire the historical marker by the old courthouse, allowing Jacqui a moment to lean against him. She rested her head on his shoulder, feeling the steadiness of his presence. It was disconcerting how natural it felt to be this close to him, how hard it was now to imagine a time when he hadn't been by her side.

With each landmark, each wave to a neighbor, Jacqui's awareness of Noah—his touch, his scent, the sound of his voice—grew stronger. She couldn't remember the last time she had walked these streets alone, nor did she want to. The thought of not having his hand to hold, his smile to meet her gaze, his laughter mingling with hers, seemed unimaginable now.

The thought made her growl. Or perhaps that was her stomach.

"Let's stop in here for a bite."

By the time Noah had pushed open the door to the establishment, it was already too late to back away. A wave of fried aromas hit them—the heavy scent of oil and batter, a stark contrast to the subtle spices and steamed offerings of Jacqui's own establishment. Jacqui instinctively wrinkled her nose, her chef's sensibilities rebelling against the pervasive smell of barbecue sauce. The interior of the restaurant was bustling with a rustic charm that was unmistakably Southern. Paper menus were scattered across the tables, signaling the ever-changing daily specials that were a hallmark of this down-home eatery. The staff milled about in casual attire, each person's unique style replacing the uniformity that Jacqui's own team adhered to.

The layout of the restaurant was open, allowing patrons a clear view straight into the kitchen. It was a noisy, lively hub where the clatter of pans and the sizzle of the grill were on full display. As Jacqui's eyes adjusted to the scene, her rival, the owner of the restaurant, caught sight of her from across the room. A broad, knowing grin spread across his face as he wiped his hands on his apron and made his way toward them and accused her of spying.

"You here to spy on how real comfort food is made?"

"Nope," she said. "Just starving, and there was a line at the gas station. So we're here."

Jedidiah Winchester chuckled, clearly enjoying the banter and the implied challenge. "Maybe you'll pick up a tip or two while you're here."

Jed's casual demeanor shifted momentarily as he did a double-take upon seeing Noah. The recognition in his eyes was unmistakable, a look Jacqui had often seen her grandfather use when he spotted a fellow veteran. It was a look that spoke of shared experiences and unspoken understanding, typically reserved for those who had served.

Noah returned Jed's look. There was a brief, silent exchange between them. Noah's expression softened, respect mingling with surprise as he nodded slightly toward Jed.

"You must be the new husband everyone's gossiping about."

"That would be me."

"Noah Henry. If memory serves, you earned the Purple Heart for—"

"It's ancient history."

Another bout of silent communication passed between the two men. Jacqui didn't like it. She especially didn't like that Jed knew more about her husband than she did. Noah had earned a medal?

"Have a seat. Try the house special. On the house, of course."

"You don't have to—" Jacqui began.

"It'll be my pleasure. I'm still smarting from that review your sister gave me the last time she was in town. That was a hit job if ever I saw one."

"Jami is always honest. If she said your chicken was dry, then it was."

"I'll prepare this plate myself so you can be the

judge until she gets back." Jed straightened the salt and pepper shakers on the table. Then rearranged the silverware. "When will that be, by the way?"

Jacqui shrugged. Not because she didn't know when her sister would be back stateside. Because she wouldn't tell this man if she did.

Jed returned to the kitchen, shouting orders and laughing with his staff. That was something Jacqui never did—laugh with her staff. Or pick up the utensils to cook a meal. Despite her initial reservations, she recognized the appeal of this place—it was unpretentious, hearty, and vibrant, a community hub that was as much about the experience as it was about the food.

"Tell me about your sisters," said Noah, drawing her attention back to him.

"Jules you met."

"The diabetic that owns a bakery shop? She likes to live dangerously."

"Mom always said to make friends with what you're afraid of. Jules grew up afraid of sugar. So she made friends with it."

"What about Jami?"

"Great cook. Amazing writer. She travels through Asia and brings back authentic recipes."

"Have you ever been?"

"To Asia?" Jacqui nodded. "A few times. But not in years, not since my parents died."

Noah reached across the table for her hand. Jacqui hadn't realized she'd let his hand go. Her fingers were drawn to his like magnets.

He didn't press her to talk about her parents' deaths. Which made her want to. But just then, the food arrived.

Jacqui found she not only enjoyed the food, she enjoyed her husband's company. He peppered her with questions about her sisters and her childhood, about Nãinai and the restaurant. He steered clear of her parents, only venturing in with the few tidbits she chose to give. By the end of the meal, Jacqui had resolved to tell him everything. But first, she wanted to know more about him.

"Tell me about you. What did you do in the military?"

Noah leaned back, a thoughtful look crossing his features. "I was an EOD tech—explosive ordnance disposal. It was my job to handle and dispose of unexploded ordnance. Bombs, essentially."

"That must be why you're so good with wires."

His smile faded. "Yeah, something like that."

Jacqui noticed a slight shift in his demeanor, a

tightening around his eyes. "Why did you leave the military?"

At her question, Noah's expression closed off, as if a shutter had been drawn over his emotions. A wall rose between them, sudden and impenetrable.

Jacqui reached across the table, her fingers brushing his. Noah's fingers flexed. She thought he was moving away from her. But his fingers began to curl around hers.

"I'm sorry," she said. "I didn't mean—"

Before she could finish, the wail of fire truck sirens sliced through the air, startling both of them. They turned instinctively toward the sound, watching through the window as red lights flashed and fire trucks roared past, heading in the direction of Chow Town.

At the same time, Jacqui's phone vibrated insistently on the table. She picked it up, her heart sinking as she read the incoming text.

"Jacqui, what is it?"

"There's been a fire at the restaurant."

CHAPTER TWENTY-NINE

The scene that unfolded before Noah was a visceral punch to the gut. The sight of it had him doubling over as he tried to draw in a breath, only to be dragged back through time and across continents. The front of Chow Town was swathed in chaos.

Fire trucks barricaded the street. Sirens wailed incessantly. Harsh, staccato bursts of radio chatter pierced the air. Flashing lights painted the scene in surreal strokes of red and blue while smoke billowed out, mingling with the sharp tang of burnt materials and the acrid bite of chemicals.

Noah moved closer, his steps uncertain, as though he suspected a live mine under the rocks in the cracked pavement. His ears filled with the familiar, unwelcome sound of his heartbeat thundering in his chest. The air was thick, not just with smoke but with the palpable tension of emergency responders moving swiftly, their shouts occasionally muffled by the masks covering their faces. Water streamed down the pavement, mixing with debris and, disturbingly, with traces of blood from minor injuries sustained during the evacuation.

It was too much. The sights, the smells, the sounds—they all merged into a grotesque echo of his last mission, the one that haunted his dreams. He had been the EOD tech on the ground, the one everyone counted on. But the bomb had been different, rigged in a way he hadn't anticipated. He had tried to defuse it, hands steady until the very moment they weren't. The explosion had been catastrophic, not just in physical damage but in the lives lost—friends and comrades who had trusted him to keep them safe.

Now standing here, it was as if the universe had cruelly dropped him back into that day. The guilt that had simmered just below his surface surged up, fierce and consuming. He couldn't breathe; he couldn't think. The guilt told him that this, too, was his fault. If he had never come to this town, would Chow Town still be standing?

"There's only superficial damage to your restaurant, Jacqui," a fireman was saying. "Just some burns in your office."

Jacqui could have been in that office if Noah hadn't driven her away from the restaurant. If he hadn't made her spend the day with him. If he hadn't threatened to kiss her in the car and then refused to let go of her hand.

Because he had done all those things, she was well. She was alive. He had to be thankful for that. But his brain still nagged him that the fire was his fault.

"It's the bakery that really took the brunt."

Tears stained Jacqui's blouse. But they weren't her tears. They belonged to her sister, who Jacqui held tightly in her arms.

From the outside, Chow Town bore only superficial scars—a bit of soot here, a water stain there—but the bakery was a different story. It looked like a wounded animal, hobbled and hurting. The bakery's large front windows, once gleaming and inviting, were now blackened and cracked, the charming display of pastries and breads replaced by the charred remains of a once-thriving business. The smell of burnt dough was heavy in the air, a bitter reminder of the disaster.

Noah's work at Chow Town had been meticulous; every wire and circuit had been given his full attention, ensuring everything met the highest safety standards. His brief work in the bakery, however, had been a different story. He'd only been asked to do a quick fix, a patchwork job that wasn't meant to be a long-term solution but just enough to keep things running until he could give the establishment his full attention.

Now as he surveyed the damage, the burned-out façade, the collapsed roof section, and the firefighters moving through the ruins, Noah felt a deep, unsettling guilt. He knew, logically, that he wasn't responsible for the bakery. He hadn't been hired to fix it fully; he hadn't been the one to make decisions about its overall safety.

Yet the *what ifs* plagued him, gnawing at his conscience. What if he had insisted on doing a complete job right away? What if his patch-job had been what failed the grid? Could he have prevented this?

The air around him was thick with smoke and the murmurs of onlookers and workers clearing debris. The sharp, acrid scent of electrical burn mingled with the sweeter, sadder smell of scorched pastry. The smell kept trying to bring him back to the past, back to when they'd pressed a medal in his hands that would never replace the loss of his friends.

"It's going to be okay. It's going to be okay."

Jacqui's words to Jules were a mantra. They slowly filtered through the haze of Noah's flashbacks, each one a lifeline thrown across the dark water of his thoughts. He took a deep, shuddering breath, tasting the coolness of the evening air rather than the hot, metallic tang of blood and explosives. He focused on Jacqui's steady presence, allowing it to pull him back from the precipice of his past.

The chief clapped Noah on the back, breaking his reverie. "You know, if it hadn't been for your work on the restaurant, this whole building would've gone down. The Chous would've lost everything."

Noah's mind flashed back to the moment he was awarded the Purple Heart. He had been heralded as a hero for saving lives, but all he could think about were those he hadn't saved. The medal had felt heavy on his chest, a reminder of the cost at which it came.

As the chief walked away to oversee the cleanup, Noah's gaze lingered on the scene. The bustle of the firefighters, the crackling of the water-soaked embers, and the distant murmur of onlookers blended into a cacophony that seemed both distant and overly loud.

Turning, Noah spotted Jacqui standing a little ways off, her face lit by the glow of the emergency vehicle lights. She was talking to one of the firefighters, her expression one of determination and strength, yet he could see the strain around her eyes, the slight tremor in her hands.

Noah felt a tug in his chest, a deep-seated need to go to her, to wrap his arms around her and reassure her that they would rebuild together. But he also felt undeserving, still haunted by the ashes of his past and the too-fresh memory of today's losses. With a heavy heart, he turned away from the scene, each step feeling like a mile.

CHAPTER THIRTY

*J*acqui wrapped a soft, fleecy blanket around Jules. Her sister tried to stifle her sobs, but she was losing the battle. Jacqui ached inside as she watched the pain of the loss hunch her baby sister's shoulders. She would do anything to take away the hurt.

But she was helpless, too. Jacqui did not do helpless well.

She headed into the kitchen to make her sister a cup of tea. The scent of smoke still lingered faintly in the air, a harsh reminder of the fire that had ravaged Jules' bakery. The devastation was complete, and the emotional toll it took on both sisters was palpable.

Tea would soothe them both. Not just any tea,

but one brewed from loose leaves, the way she had been taught, steeped in tradition by her father and grandfather.

However, in the quiet of the kitchen, Jacqui's hands shook as she opened the bag of tea leaves. The delicate leaves scattered clumsily into the pot rather than the graceful dance they were meant to perform.

Every motion was haunted by the ghost of her past. Jacqui had been the one to prepare the last meal for her mother before she was taken by cancer. She'd done the same for her father the night before he died. His heart had simply given out without the love of his life by his side.

The last meals she had prepared for her parents —those final acts of love had become tangled in her memory with loss and finality. Since then, her own kitchen had seen no cooking. Her skills and passion lay dormant, buried under the weight of her grief.

This brew was the furthest she'd gotten in a recipe in years. As the leaves swirled in the steaming water, her attempts at control unraveled. It was then that Nāinai stepped quietly into the kitchen.

With a knowing look, her grandmother observed Jacqui's struggle. Without a word, she placed her aged, steady hand over Jacqui's trembling one. The contact was grounding, a gentle but firm reminder of family and support that had always been the backbone of their lives.

Nãinai took over, her movements sure and practiced. She finished preparing the tea, her hands skillfully coaxing the leaves to release their flavor. The smell of jasmine tea filled the air, blending with the faint scent of smoke that seemed to have followed them from the restaurant.

"The fire chief said it could have been much worse," Jacqui told Jules when she handed her the cup, trying to infuse some hope into the grim atmosphere. "He said the new wiring Noah did in Chow Town actually helped prevent the fire from spreading."

"That young man has good hands and a good heart," Nãinai said as she stirred her tea.

Jacqui's gaze wandered to the window, her thoughts drifting to Noah. She hadn't seen him since they left the scene. He must have gone back to the bakery to help with cleanup efforts. It was just like him to think of others, to put himself where he was most needed without a second thought for his own rest or comfort.

She saw a figure moving in the dark. A broad-shouldered man. Her heart leapt at the thought of Noah. She rushed to the door. But when she pulled it open, it wasn't Noah.

"I just came to check on Jules," said Fish.

Jacqui stepped aside to let the big man in. "I thought you were Noah."

"I thought he was here." Fish's gaze went to Jules. He scanned her as though he was looking her over for injuries and wounds. But Jules hadn't been at the bakery when the fire had happened.

"Why don't you try to get some rest, Jules? There's a new bed in the guest room, fresh sheets too. It might help to lie down for a bit."

Jules shook her head. "I have too much to do. I need to talk to the fire chief. I need to start getting estimates and—"

"I can do that," said Jacqui.

"No. It's my business. It's my responsibility."

"You're my responsibility."

Jules threw off the blanket and slammed down the tea cup. "Jacqui, I'm a grown woman, not a kid. You need to stop treating me like a sick child and go and live your own life. You need to stop dogging Jami's every step while she's an ocean away, and focus on you."

Jacqui jerked back like her sister had slapped her.

Her hands, still slightly trembling from earlier, now hung limply at her sides. The shock of hearing such blunt rejection from Jules, whose well-being had always been a central pillar in her life, left her speechless.

She swallowed hard, the lump in her throat growing with each breath. She had always seen her actions as supportive, the natural duties of an older sister looking out for her family. The idea that her sisters might view her care as overbearing or intrusive was jarring. Her intentions, pure and protective in her mind, were now painted as meddling and suffocating.

Tears pricked the corners of her eyes, blurring her vision slightly. She blinked them back, not wanting to appear even more overbearing or emotional. But the hurt was there, undeniable and sharp, cutting through her like the knives she had once so expertly wielded in her kitchen.

Jules hopped up off the couch and wrapped her arms around Jacqui. It wasn't the first time her sister had given her a hug. But it was the first time the hug was meant to comfort Jacqui and not the other way around. Admittedly, Jacqui didn't know how to receive the affection.

"I know you care, Jacks, I do. But I need to handle this myself. I need to know I can."

Jacqui heard her sister's words, but she wasn't processing. What if Jules missed a detail and something went wrong? What if she tried to do something kind, something to show her affection and someone didn't wake up in the morning?

"I shouldn't have waited for you to hire someone to redo the electrical on the bakery. I should've done it myself. That was my fault."

"I said I would—"

Jules squeezed Jacqui tighter, cutting off whatever she would've said next. "When you hover like this, you suffocate me."

Jacqui's hands trembled against her baby sister's back. She warred with the need to pull her close, though at the same time to push her away.

"And then when things go wrong, you feel guilty about it, and I'm not even thinking about it."

Now Jacqui's hands went lax as they slid down Jules' back to land at her side. Jules let go and tilted her head back to look at her sister.

"I love that you're there for me. I'll never stop needing you. But I need to be in charge of my life."

Jacqui nodded slowly, her mind racing as she processed this shift in their dynamic. It was a painful realization, seeing the gap between her intentions and her actions through her sister's eyes. Because Jules was right, Jacqui was feeling guilty over something that wasn't her fault. Her first instinct was to not let Jules near a kitchen again. Just like she'd mostly stayed out of the kitchens after her parents' deaths.

"I would like to help you with the repairs."

Both Chou sisters turned to Fish. Jacqui had forgotten the man was there. Which was funny since he took up so much space in her living room.

"With what money?" huffed Jules. "I'm sure the insurance will point to the faulty wiring."

"I'll work for free," said Fish.

"I would never take advantage of you like that. And even if I had no scruples, we need supplies. And Mr. Pettigrew won't open up his hardware store as a charity."

Fish opened his mouth to speak again, likely to offer to give Jules the world. Or worse, to rob the local bank for her. Jacqui hadn't missed the way her sous chef had looked at her baby sister this past year.

"We have the money." Jules' gaze swung to Nāinai, who sat with her teacup in her hands watching the events unfold. "You need to release my inheritance money, Nāinai."

"I can't change my husband's will. You know the only way to get that money is to marry."

"Then I'll marry her."

Once again, all the Chou women turned to gape at Fish.

CHAPTER THIRTY-ONE

*N*oah sat in the dimly lit room, the only light a flicker from the streetlamp outside casting long shadows across the floor. He turned the Purple Heart medal over in his hands, its weight familiar yet foreign.

The medal had once seared his skin with its burden. He'd rarely picked it up, each touch a reminder of what he had lost. Now it lay cool and inert in his palm, a contradiction to the fire it stirred within him. The medal called him a hero. The title rang hollow.

He'd lost friends, brothers and sisters in arms, on the day he earned this honor. Their faces sometimes blurred in his memory, but their voices, their laughter, were as clear as if they were in the room with him. Each loss was a ghost that lingered, whispering of what might have been if only he'd been a little faster, a little smarter, a little better.

And yet, he had saved lives too—many lives. Lives that had gone on to embrace loved ones. To live out dreams. To make marks on the world.

Noah could almost feel the fire chief's hand on his back earlier that day. The chief's grip and been a firm, grateful pressure that spoke of lives continued because of his work on the restaurant. It should have felt good, validating. People inside Chow Town had been bruised but not broken, scared but safe. It could have been much worse had he not done the rewiring.

But was it enough?

In the stillness of the dark room, Noah let out a long, weary sigh, the sound heavy with fatigue and introspection. He leaned back in the chair, the creak of the wood a sharp punctuation in the quiet. The dichotomy of his emotions—the pride and the guilt, the honor and the horror—wrestled within him like a storm.

Noah closed his eyes, trying to reconcile the parts of himself that felt irreparably fractured. The

Purple Heart in his hand didn't make the answers any clearer, nor did it ease the burden he carried. But as he sat there, enveloped by the night, he realized that maybe it wasn't about being enough by some intangible standard. Maybe it was about doing what he could, when he could, with all the strength and skill he had.

Tomorrow, he would rise and do it all again. He'd fix what was broken. He'd help where he could. And maybe, just maybe, he'd start to believe that he could mend the breaks within himself too.

A soft sigh escaped from Jacqui's lips. The sound sliced through the silence in her bedroom—their bedroom. He'd tried to leave town, but he couldn't. Not when his heart resided here.

In her sleep, Jacqui murmured a name. He leaned in to feel the exhale of the name against his upper lip. He could do that because she was his wife, and she had whispered his name in her sleep. Her hand stretched across the cool sheets of the bed, reaching for him, her fingers grasping at the empty space where he should have been.

Noah watched her, the moonlight casting a silver glow across her peaceful face. She seemed to be searching for him even in her dreams, pulling him in like a siren's call. It was a reminder of why he hadn't been able to drive away earlier that night. After sitting in his car, keys in hand, the image of Jacqui's face had anchored him, pulling him back to his new reality. The world could explode around him, but he would stand in its center if that's where his wife was.

Noah set the medal down on the nightstand and quietly slipped into the bed beside Jacqui. He reached out, taking her searching hand in his, interlocking their fingers. The contact soothed her instantly. Her hand gripped his with a gentle strength, pulling herself closer to him.

Jacqui's eyes fluttered open. The haziness of sleep clouded her gaze. When she saw him, a slow, radiant smile spread across her face, illuminating the room more than any light could. "Noah, you're home."

He was. He was home. Not because he was in this bed. If she had slept in another bed, he would destroy this one and come to that one.

He wanted to tell her about his struggles of the day, his struggles of the past. He would. But not now. Right now, he didn't want any struggle. All that would be between him and the woman he loved would be surrender.

"Are you okay?" Jacqui ran her fingers over his brow, straightening out the crease she found there.

Noah nuzzled into her touch, seeking her warmth and care. "Seeing that fire was tough."

"You know that wasn't your fault."

"Do you?"

Her grin told him *check mate.* "Jules wouldn't let me take the blame. Or the responsibility to fix it."

"I'll help her rebuild."

"Me, too. I promised my sister I wouldn't try to take over. But that doesn't mean I won't still be by her side the whole way... double checking to make sure everything is done correctly."

In the darkness, Noah grinned at his wife. She was learning to let go, but she'd never abandon those she cared about.

"Seeing that fire, it brought back some bad memories. Of my time in the service."

"You want to talk about it?"

"Not tonight, but I will tell you. I won't ever keep secrets from you. Again."

"Again?"

"I lied to you, Jacqui. But I think you know I did."

Noah looked into his wife's beautiful face. He could see her clearly in the darkness of the bedroom. Her eyes sparkled at him, even though they weren't fighting.

"I never had any intention of ending this marriage," he said.

The light in her eyes turned into a full blaze.

"I love you. I think I fell in love with you the first time you snapped at me."

Tears welled in Jacqui's eyes, but they didn't put out the flame.

"I'm going to spend the rest of my life fighting with you, fighting for you. I'm going to be your hero because you rescued me."

"You rescued me, too. You rescued me from myself. I got so used to doing everything, carrying all the weight. Until you."

Noah pressed his mouth to her temple. Then to the corner of her right eye. He repeated the gesture at the corner of her left eye.

"You make me feel light and free. You make me feel like I can fly. Though my sisters want me to stop hovering over them."

Noah pulled his wife on top of him. "I don't want you to stop hovering over me."

"Good, because I have no intention of letting you go."

He leaned in, his lips meeting hers in a kiss that sealed his silent promise—a promise to stay, to love, and to be there, always. Jacqui's kiss warmed Noah from the inside out. The doubts and the shadows of his past might never fully disappear, but with Jacqui, he had a reason to face them, to fight through them. Here, with her, he found his resolve, his purpose, and his home.

CHAPTER THIRTY-TWO

"*I*t smells amazing in here." Noah's voice was a soothing rumble in her ear as he came into the kitchen. "Did my wife cook her husband breakfast?"

"She did." Jacqui paused, her hand on the spatula stilling as she leaned back into his embrace.

It was just an omelet: two eggs scrambled with some spices. But it was another leap forward in their relationship. Jacqui had confided in Noah about making both her parents' last meals. He had listened without prejudice or censure. He'd placed his hand at her low back as she'd mixed a homemade remoulade sauce for the fish sticks they'd had last night.

Now Noah's arms tightened around her, his

presence a solid comfort. There was a sacredness to the moment, a tender vulnerability in Jacqui's admission that made the kitchen—the heart of her home—feel like a confessional. The sizzle of the omelet in the pan punctuated her words, a reminder of life continuing around them, relentless and demanding despite the memories that haunted both of them.

He had told her about his last mission when things hadn't gone as planned. He'd confessed his guilt, his shame. She hadn't tried to absolve him of blame. She'd simply sat by him and held his hand in hers as he'd whispered his innermost secrets to her.

Then he'd held on to her like she was his lifeline. She'd kissed him like he was an oasis in a desert. They hadn't made it upstairs to their bedroom. Instead, they'd stumbled into the guest room and made use of the bed in there. They'd nearly broken it in their passion for one another.

Now Noah's fingers caressed her wrist as she flipped the omelet. "I bet it's delicious."

Jacqui took a deep breath, drawing in the mingling scents of spices and the comforting smell of Noah's cologne. She slid the omelet onto a plate, its colors vibrant with herbs and the edges perfectly crisped. It had been a couple of years since she'd made anything from scratch. But it had been like riding a bike.

She'd infused the omelet with the Asian spices of her childhood. Every now and then, her hand had trembled slightly as she'd cracked an egg over the hot pan or maneuvered the spatula to fold the eggs gently. But it had turned out perfectly.

Setting the plate down in front of Noah at the kitchen table, Jacqui brushed her hands nervously on her apron, watching him with a mix of anticipation and apprehension. Every emotion played across her face as she waited for him to take the first bite. Her heart caught in her throat. This wasn't just about the food; it was about letting someone in, about healing and sharing life again, meal by meal.

Noah lifted his fork, breaking into the omelet and bringing a piece to his mouth. He chewed thoughtfully, his eyes closing briefly as he savored the taste. When he opened them, his expression was one of pure appreciation.

Then his expression suddenly changed. His eyes widened. A moment later, he began to cough lightly. Then a bit more forcefully as he waved a hand in front of his open mouth.

"Oh, no. Is it too spicy?" Jacqui leapt into action, her previous anxiety switching to concern. She rushed to the fridge, pouring him a glass of milk and bringing it over to the table.

Noah took the glass with a nod of thanks, gulping down the milk in a few quick swallows. He set the glass down, still fanning his mouth with his hand.

"Wow, that's got some kick to it," he managed to say, his voice slightly hoarse.

Jacqui bit her lip, suppressing a nervous giggle. "I'm so sorry. I might have gotten a bit carried away with the spice."

"Maybe a kiss from my beautiful wife will do the trick."

"I thought my kisses usually got you heated."

She leaned down, and their lips met in a loving kiss. Noah's lips were warm and a touch spicy, but not enough to cause Jacqui any discomfort. The kiss was soft and sweet, carrying with it the promise of countless breakfasts and late night desserts to come.

Pulling away, Jacqui looked into Noah's eyes, her smile radiant. "Did that help?" she asked, her voice low and soft.

Noah's response was to pull her in for another kiss, this one deeper and filled with gratitude and affection. "It's the perfect blend of sweet and spicy. You're the only heat I need, Jacqui Henry."

. . .

**Get ready for Fish and Jules story in
The Oath Operation!**

*When a beautiful baker needs a fake husband to get
her inheritance, the small town beast offers her a
sweet deal.*

I'm a big, gruff, rough around the edges beast, but
after leaving the military, all the fight went out of
me. Until the day Jules Chou, a petite diabetic baker,
put a sugar free muffin in my hand.

I instantly developed a sweet tooth for her, but this
beauty already has a prince of a boyfriend; a clean
cut, high pedigree doctor. He's perfect for her, where
there's more than just dirt under my fingernails.

When Jules needs to get married in order to gain her
inheritance and rebuild the bakery of her dreams,
Prince Charming balks insisting it's too early in his
five year plan for rings.

That's when I volunteer for service. The idiot
actually thinks he can trust me to temporarily marry

Jules and then divorce her after she gets her
inheritance.

But once I have my ring on her finger, I have no plan
to let her go. I just need to prove to her that this
beast can love her better than a prince.

**The *Oath Operation* is a sizzling, sweet romance
with no steam. The damsels agree to a marriage of
convenience, but the heroes have no intentions of
letting them out of the agreement—ever.**

ALSO BY SHANAE JOHNSON

Shanae Johnson was raised by Saturday Morning cartoons and After School Specials. She still doesn't understand why there isn't a life lesson that ties the issues of the day together just before bedtime. While she's still waiting for the meaning of it all, she writes stories to try and figure it all out. Her books are wholesome and sweet, but her are heroes are hot and heroines are full of sass!

And by the way, the E elongates the A. So it's pronounced Shan-aaaaaaaa. Perfect for a hero to call out across the moors, or up to a balcony, or to blare outside her window on a boombox. If you hear him calling her name, please send him her way!

You can sign up for Shanae's Reader Group and receive a FREE NOVELLA at

https://shanaejohnson.com/ReaderGroup

ALSO BY SHANAE JOHNSON

The Marriage Mission series

Marriage Mission

Oath Operation

Tactically Tied

Shotgun Spouse

The Betrothal Blitz

Enlisted Engagement

The Brides of Purple Heart

On His Bended Knee

Hand Over His Heart

Offering His Arm

His Permanent Scar

Having His Back

In Over His Head

Always On His Mind

Every Step He Takes

In His Good Hands

Light Up His Life

Strength to Stand

His Grace Under Pressure

The Rangers of Purple Heart

The Rancher takes his Convenient Bride

The Rancher takes his Best Friend's Sister

The Rancher takes his Runaway Bride

The Rancher takes his Star Crossed Love

The Rancher takes his Love at First Sight

The Rancher takes his Last Chance at Love

The Silver Star Ranch Romances

His Pledge to Honor

His Pledge to Cherish

His Pledge to Protect

His Pledge to Obey

His Pledge to Have

His Pledge to Hold

a Flying Cross Ranch Romance

His Vow to Love

His Vow to Treasure

His Vow to Adore

His Vow to Trust

His Vow to Respect

His Vow to Defend

Bronze Star Ranch Romance

His Duty to Serve

His Duty to Accept

His to Fulfill

9 798227 866011